AN ECLAIR TO REMEMBER

RICH AMOOI

To Silvi.
I love you.
Truly. Madly. Deeply.

CHAPTER ONE

"I'm not going to be your Rose and I don't want you to be my Jack," said Alexa.

Wonderful. Another Titanic reference. Soon she'll be quoting Elsa from Frozen.

Oscar Martin placed ten pairs of socks in his open suitcase on the bed and glanced over at his fiancée. She wasn't packing for their cruise to Alaska. Her empty suitcase sat right where he had left it at the foot of the bed. Not a good sign, since this was the trip he'd hoped would rekindle their romance. It was strange trying to salvage their relationship while she planned their wedding.

"Hollywood didn't make *Titanic* as a form of entertainment," Alexa continued. "It was a public service announcement. They were warning us that if we were crazy enough to take one of those cruises we would most likely die a horrifying death."

It wasn't the first time Alexa had an excuse for not wanting to go on vacation with Oscar. When he had mentioned Cancun to her earlier in the year she had said there was no way she would go. Then she shared info regarding the hurricane-to-death ratio.

"Do you know how cold the water is in Alaska?" she asked.

"Ice cold."

"No. Colder!"

Oscar ran his fingers through his hair. "This is a brand new ship. It's the most technologically advanced vessel on the planet."

"It's also the inaugural sailing. Why not let them go back and forth from Alaska a few thousand times to make sure it's working properly?"

"It's not necessary."

"You don't know that."

Actually, he did. Oscar knew everything about transportation. It was his job. He had hundreds of patents involving trains, boats, and airplanes. He had invented a car that hovered. Because of his knowledge of transportation, he'd been interviewed on major television news programs across the country. He'd even been a guest on *Ellen* and *The Bachelor*.

Alexa sighed. "There are volcanoes in Alaska, too. Do you know how hot that lava is?"

"Burning hot."

"No. Hotter!"

Oscar was certain her behavior today had nothing to

do with the fear of dying while on vacation. It was the wedding. Alexa had become obsessed with it. It was all she thought about, all she talked about.

Oscar remembered that she'd once had other hobbies and interests—or at least she'd said she did. This complete fixation on the wedding was, ironically, one of the reasons why he was on the verge of calling it off. She'd changed, and not for the better. He was worried about what their marriage might be like and all she cared about was the one day.

All of her Facebook posts were about the wedding—ten to fifteen a day. She had even asked her maid of honor to get spray-tanned for the wedding day because Alexa thought she'd be "too white" for the pictures. It wasn't a surprise that all of her friends had suddenly become super busy and weren't returning her phone calls.

Alexa made Bridezilla look like Mary Poppins.

Oscar stopped packing for a moment. "Why don't you tell me what this is really about?"

She grabbed the wedding magazine from the nightstand and flipped through the pages, stopping to show Oscar a picture of a cake. "This baker in Chester, England created a wedding cake with four thousand diamonds on it."

He leaned in closer to inspect the photo. "Why would anyone want four thousand diamonds on a wedding cake?"

She looked at him like he was crazy. "Because it's beautiful!"

He nodded. "Of course." Oscar was happy with the

cake they had chosen at the tasting a few weeks ago. He pointed to the magazine. "Are you telling me you want a fifty-three million dollar wedding cake?"

"Of course not," she answered, her voice going up a few octaves. "I'm saying we need to re-evaluate. I want our wedding to be on the cover of *People* magazine and *The New York Times*. I want a wedding so big and glamorous it will make Princess Di's wedding look like a backyard pizza party."

Oscar blinked. "And why do you want this?"

"Why do I want this? Why do *I* want this? What a question! It's the American dream."

"I thought owning a home was the American dream."

"*After* the American wedding! Nothing is more important than the wedding. Nothing."

What about our love? Our happiness? Or my sanity?

Oscar didn't look forward to the *I told you so* he would get from his best friend. Leo Grant was the cruise director of the new ship and had given this vacation to Oscar and Alexa as an engagement present. Leo was convinced they were incompatible and predicted Oscar would be going on the cruise by himself. Leo also thought Oscar was making a mistake by marrying Alexa.

You're settling.

Not the words you wanted to hear from your best friend. Your best man. But Oscar realized that maybe Leo was right. That's why he'd decided that this trip would be the last chance to save their relationship. To get their passion back. Because it was gone, and he missed it.

He continued to pack, neatly folding and placing four pairs of pants in the suitcase. "This cruise is a special gift from my best friend. In my culture nobody would reject a gift like this."

Alexa pushed the suitcase over and sat on the edge of the bed. "We're in the US, not Spain. Your culture doesn't count here."

Oscar was tempted to mention the Spanish influence in the United States but let it go. After all, that wasn't really the point. Yes, it would be rude not to take advantage of the gift his friend had given them, but the real problem was that his fiancée didn't seem to like any of the same things he liked, or value their relationship outside of the high-society wedding he could give her.

"Alexa, I really want you to come. It's important to me."

Alexa sighed. "But I don't want to. Why can't you just go without me?"

He sat on the edge of the bed next to her. "Why would you want me to go without you?"

"Honestly, I can get more done with you out of my hair. *And* it'll be good for you. Take your camera."

This is what gave him conflicted feelings. When it sounded like she cared. She sounded like the old Alexa he liked.

He twisted around and pulled out his little point-and-click digital camera from the suitcase, showing her. "Already packed."

"You know what I mean." She went to the closet and

fished out his camera bag from the floor underneath his suits. She returned and plopped it on his lap. "Here."

Inside that bag was his pride and joy, his Canon Rebel camera, along with memory cards, batteries, lenses, and flashes. It's not like he hadn't thought of bringing it along. Oscar loved shooting with that camera. He'd taken some award-winning shots during his South American tour that had ended up in *National Geographic* and *Smithsonian* magazines. That was over ten years ago, right before his life unexpectedly changed course. Things were much different now. He'd lost his passion for photography.

Oscar pointed to his suitcase. "I don't have space."

She leaned in and inspected the inside of his suitcase. "Do you need all of those socks?"

"You never know."

"Then carry it on."

When Oscar and Alexa had first met she had said she would love to travel. That was one of the things he loved about her because he was adventurous and wanted to see the world. In fact, most of the things he loved about her she didn't do anymore. Sometimes he wondered if she'd just been making things up to get him to propose to her, but he knew that was a terrible thing to think about someone. She'd just changed, that was all, like people do. It was like she just flicked off a switch once she got the engagement ring on her finger.

Well, maybe she had and maybe she hadn't, but the fact was that Oscar was pretty close to flipping his own switch. He needed to make her understand that if she didn't come on this trip with him, he doubted very much that they had enough in common to build a future together. He had to tell her that this cruise was a deal breaker. She deserved to know how much it mattered before she made her final decision.

"Alexa, we need to—"

She checked her watch. "Later. I've got to run."

"This is important."

"So is my bikini wax." She grabbed her purse, pulled out her lipstick and puckered for the mirror as she applied it.

"Alexa . . ."

"No. Later." She kissed him on the cheek and disappeared out the door.

Oscar walked to the bathroom and stared at his cheek in the mirror. That was another thing she didn't do anymore. Kiss on the lips. Pecks on the cheeks were supposed to be reserved for family members and friends. The truth was the lipstick on his cheek had more permanence than their relationship. He shook his head and wiped it off his face.

He returned to packing and placed his swim trunks in the suitcase. Leo had told him the ship had an amazing indoor pool and several hot tubs.

Alaska was one of the most scenic destinations in the world. Seventeen out of twenty of the tallest mountains in North America were in Alaska. The state had over a hundred thousand glaciers. The untamed and untouched wilderness and wildlife were a photographer's paradise.

No way he was going to skip the trip.

He waited for a voice to pop in his head telling him not to go. It never came.

A few seconds later, he closed the suitcase and latched it shut. He slid it off the bed so it stood upright on the floor. Then he grabbed the camera bag and secured it to the top of the suitcase.

He shook his head sadly. "Looks like someone is going to Alaska by himself."

Sydney St. James logged off the company system and shut down her laptop. The screen went dark and she slid the laptop into her computer bag. It had been a long day at work and she was glad she could finally go home and pack.

She smiled thinking of the cruise to Alaska. She'd worked harder than everyone in her department as senior administrative assistant, so the vacation was well deserved. It was also mandatory. A company memo went out last month stating their new use-it-or-lose-it vacation policy. She had six weeks of accumulated vacation time built up and had until the end of the year to use it or it would disappear. She had no problem with that. The cruise with her best friend Gina, plus the time off for the European honeymoon with her fiancé Elliot would take care of those six weeks.

Sydney's cell rang and she pulled it out from her purse. It was Gina.

"I'm leaving the office now."

"Why are you still there?" asked Gina. "You need to get home and pack. We're going to Alaska!"

Sydney laughed. It was odd hearing her best friend excited about the cruise, considering all she'd done over the last few weeks was complain about it. This trip was Sydney's bachelorette party and Gina had originally wanted to go to Vegas. Sydney nixed that idea as soon as it came out of Gina's mouth and told her best friend it was Alaska or nothing. Unfortunately, none of Sydney's other friends could get the time off, so this was a two-girl bachelorette party.

She had always wanted to visit The Last Frontier and write about the adventure. The only reason she could get a cabin on the sold-out cruise was because of her connection to the travel industry. Before her admin position, she'd been a travel agent and had a popular blog where she had written about her adventures around the world.

She was excited but then was presented with another dilemma. Her fiancé hated cold weather. If she didn't go to Alaska before she got married she would probably never go. This was it. She had to admit that turning the cruise into her bachelorette party had been a brilliant idea. Still, hearing Gina excited about Alaska didn't make sense at all. Something was up.

"Are you drunk?" asked Sydney.

Gina laughed. "No! Why would you ask such a silly question?"

"Just yesterday you were still complaining about the cruise. So what happened in the last twenty-four hours that made you change your mind?"

"Google."

"Ahh. Of course."

Gina's answer to everything was Google. New recipe? Google. Mysterious rash on the back of the hand? Google. Gina had even Googled Google on Google.

Sydney straightened out her desk calendar and pushed her chair under her desk. "What did you find out?"

"This cruise is going to be insane! Everybody is talking about it. Five star meals, top shelf drinks, plus Hollywood celebrities. I'd love to have a picture with Colin Farrell or Bradley Cooper."

"They'll be on the cruise?"

"You never know! It would be cool to meet a big time celebrity."

"Whatever floats your boat."

Gina screamed. "Good one!"

Sydney held the phone away from her ear for a moment and sighed. "It feels odd not being able to talk to Elliot before I go."

"That's what you get when your fiancé is a workaholic."

Elliot's position of vice president of sales required him to travel around the world. He was home only two weekends out of the entire month. The problem with that was he wasn't motivated to do anything—especially travel —when he was home or when his vacation came around. She felt lonely sometimes. But he promised it would get better once he was promoted to president of sales. In two years. She wasn't sure how that was possible with an even more demanding position.

Sydney sighed. "I think I'm getting cold feet."

"Put on some socks."

"Seriously. I know Elliot isn't the man I've always dreamed of, but that man probably doesn't exist, right?"

"I can't answer that."

"Elliot's a nice guy."

"No argument there. And hot as hell. Personally, I wouldn't be able to handle a man who was never around. I need that closeness, that intimacy. I want kisses every day. Spooning. Sticking my cold feet under his legs at night in bed . . ."

Sydney wanted that, too.

Gina laughed. "You see *me* way more than you see him. Hey, you and I should get married instead!"

Sydney smiled. "You're my soulmate."

"*That* is the truth."

Sidney grabbed her computer bag and purse to head out when someone cleared his throat behind her.

She turned around slowly, certain of who she would find.

Jake. Her boss.

The man had a bad habit of adding something new to her to-do list right when she was on her way out for the evening. He did it at least a couple of times a week and, judging by the folder in his hand, he was ready to do it again.

"Before you take off . . . ," he said.

"Is that Jake?" asked Gina, still on the phone. "No, no, no. Don't let him give you a new project now. Tell him to stick it up his—"

Sydney hung up on Gina and forced a smile. "What's up, Jake? I'm heading out for my vacation, remember?"

"I know and I hate to do this to you, but it's important."

It always is.

She sat her computer bag and purse on her chair and stared at the folder. "What is it?"

He handed her the folder. "I need you to call these vendors for the conference and find out their status with the giveaways. I never got email confirmation from them and marketing needs to know if their names are going on the banners or not."

She opened the folder and flipped through the pages. "Many of them are on the East Coast. Their offices are closed. Can't this wait until the morning?"

"You won't be here in the morning and I'll be on the golf course. Anyway, they'll get your voicemail first thing. And send them each an email saying you've left an urgent voicemail. Thanks."

He disappeared before she could say anything else.

She pulled her laptop out of the case and powered it

back up. She dropped her purse on the floor, slid into her chair, and sighed.

She was grateful to have a job that paid well, but it didn't fulfill her emotionally. They took advantage of her and it wasn't fair. It also created a lot of stress in her life.

Sydney wanted to do something she was passionate about.

Traveling was her passion and she couldn't wait to be on the ship with Gina. The last cruise she went on was over three years ago through the Panama Canal. It was an amazing experience she had written about on her blog, but she had come home to no job. Her life had changed dramatically when the travel agency closed and she stopped traveling.

She opened up the folder and got to work. By this time tomorrow she would be on a cruise and all would be good.

Thirty seconds later, her phone rang. Gina again.

Sydney answered the call. "Yes, I'm still at work."

"No!" screamed Gina, forcing Sydney to hold the phone away from her ear again. "Stress is unhealthy. You better not get sick on the trip."

"Don't be so dramatic."

"I'm serious, you need to be careful. My mom's best friend was in the hospital for a week because of stress. Give me Jake's address. I'll pay him a little visit."

Sydney laughed. "You sound like Robert De Niro."

"Promise me you're going home soon."

"I promise."

"Good. Because you're going on vacation tomorrow

and you'll come home a new person. It will change your life!"

She appreciated Gina's enthusiasm, but doubted very much that a cruise could have that much impact on a person's life. It was just a cruise. A vacation. What could possibly happen that could change her life?

CHAPTER TWO

Oscar finished unpacking in the Denali Suite and stepped out onto his private balcony on the ship. He took in a deep breath of the fresh Pacific Ocean air and sat on one of the cushiony lounge chairs. The sail away from San Francisco was breathtaking as they cruised past Alcatraz, underneath the Golden Gate Bridge, and up the northern California coast. They would be at sea for two days before arriving in their first port of call, Ketchikan, Alaska. It was odd that Alexa wasn't there, but this trip would definitely be good for him.

A few moments later, the sound of the doorbell got him back on his feet. He headed inside the suite toward the entryway and swung the door open. "Leo!"

His best friend stepped inside, looking sharp in his navy blue blazer with a red tie. He had a nametag on his chest and carried a clipboard with a pen hooked on top.

Leo hugged Oscar and squeezed his arm. "Welcome, my friend."

Oscar pointed to Leo's spiked black hair. It was shorter than usual. "Fancy haircut."

Leo shrugged. "An inaugural cruise is a big deal. I have to look good for the pictures, you know. I trust the living arrangements are satisfactory?"

Oscar chuckled. "This suite is so big it comes with a doorbell. How many square feet are we talking here?"

Leo closed the door behind him. "Fourteen hundred, not counting the five hundred square foot balcony."

"And how did you swing this? I know you didn't pay for it."

"You're a wise man. You're also Oscar Martin—the world's *second* sexiest man alive."

"So David Beckham wasn't available?"

Leo shook his head. "He had to attend a wedding. You're better looking than him anyway. At least you don't have a man bun."

Oscar chuckled. "Maybe that's why he won."

"They gave him extra points for marrying a Spice Girl."

"Shouldn't that be minus points? Anyway, thanks for the suite. It wasn't necessary, but thank you."

"You're welcome, but the publicity we'll get from you cruising with us will be worth a hundred times more than the cost of the suite. So basically, I'm using you."

"I can appreciate that. How's the new job?"

"Like a dream. I was born to be a cruise director, I'm

telling ya. I'm in my element. Being around people is my passion."

Oscar couldn't argue with that. Leo was the head of hospitality at Stanford when they had first met many years ago. His friend had gone out of his way to introduce himself at one of the campus restaurants and he'd made Oscar feel welcome. That had meant a lot to Oscar since he'd just arrived from Spain and didn't know a single person. They'd hit it off immediately and had become best friends. Oscar had missed Leo when he'd left Stanford to work in the hotel industry, but they had always stayed in touch.

"I like seeing you happy," said Oscar. "And you deserve it."

"Hey, you deserve happiness, too. Everybody does."

Leo was always positive, another thing Oscar liked about him. He had even admitted he'd been jealous of Leo's happiness. Oscar had many things . . . money, fame, success, a beautiful fiancée. Still, something was missing.

He glanced over at his camera bag on the bar stool and wondered if that something missing was located inside the bag.

Leo followed his eyes to the camera bag. "You brought it!"

"Doesn't mean I'll use it."

"Hey, baby steps. I have a good feeling about this." Leo smirked. "Even if you didn't bring your fiancée."

"I wondered how long it would take you to mention it. You didn't seem surprised when you entered."

Leo grinned. "I have access to all of our passengers' information."

"Well, it's over between us."

"Also not a surprise. She was using you. When did you break it off?"

"Technically, I haven't. I tried before I left but she wouldn't let me speak."

"Another shocker."

"She had an important bikini wax appointment."

Leo laughed. "Okay, let's forget about that. It's going to be an amazing trip. You're getting ready to go to the buffet, correct?"

"How did you know?"

"I told you—I know everything. You were smart to wait until now to go. The buffet is a complete madhouse on the first night. You'd think these people haven't eaten in a week. Enjoy and I'll look for you later. I need to check in on the bingo room and make sure everything is ready to go."

"Sounds good. And hey . . ."

Leo opened the door to leave and turned around. "Yeah?"

"You were right about Alexa, but thank you for not saying *I told you so.*"

Leo let the door close and approached Oscar, hugging him. Then he slapped him on the side of the arm. "Everything will work out just fine."

A few minutes later, Oscar was out the door and heading upstairs to dinner. Halfway up the stairs he passed an older couple and heard the woman say, "That's Oscar Martin."

He was used to the attention and didn't make a big deal about it.

At the top of the steps, a steward smiled. "Good evening, Mr. Martin. All settled in?"

"Yes. Thank you."

He continued toward the buffet and wondered how many people out of the four thousand on board he would talk to. This trip was supposed to be relaxing, right?

He laughed at the thought. He had no problem engaging with people. He enjoyed being social, although not as much as Leo. But it was expected from a guy always in the public eye.

He continued toward the food area and—

"Oscar Martin!" said the woman, dragging a man by the wrist in his direction. "I thought that was you. What a pleasure. I'm Joanne and this is my husband Raymond."

"A pleasure to meet you both."

They were an older couple, most likely retired like some of the other passengers onboard.

"The pleasure is all mine." Joanne winked at Oscar. "And you should have beat David Beckham. The man needs a haircut." She pulled her husband closer. "Raymond, I want you to take a look at Oscar."

Raymond eyed Oscar from top to bottom. "Okay."

"Are you looking at him?"

"I'm looking, Joanne."

"What do you see?"

Raymond shrugged. "Oscar Martin."

"No. Go deeper into his effervescence—the man's got viscosity."

"You're telling me he's thick and sticky in consistency due to internal friction?"

"What? No! Okay, I must be using the wrong word."

"I think you are, dear."

Oscar laughed and wondered if he needed to be there for this conversation.

Joanne frowned. "Okay, forget what I said. But can you see the passion oozing from Oscar's body?"

Raymond eyed him up and down again. "I can."

Joanne pushed her husband closer to Oscar. "Don't be scared. Get a good look."

Raymond wiggled his nose. "He smells nice."

"Quit doing that. You look like a rabbit." She turned to Oscar. "Do you think you can help my husband, Oscar?"

"In what way?"

"He needs some of your passion. He doesn't have any."

Raymond stuck his hands in his pockets and stared at his feet. "She's right."

"You'd be a great passion surrogate."

He hadn't heard that one before. "Unfortunately, I don't have time." Oscar pointed toward the buffet. "I'm going to grab some food, if you don't mind."

"I understand completely. Passion burns calories—you must be starving. We'll talk later."

Oscar arrived at the buffet and stopped. Leo was right; it was insane. People scrambling for food like it was their last meal on earth. He watched a man collide with a woman, both trying to get a slice of pizza. An employee wiped up a spill in front of the soft drink machines and another man carried three plates filled with food back to his table. He suddenly lost his appetite.

The hostess took a couple of steps toward Oscar. "Good evening, Mr. Martin. We have a reserved table ready for you."

Oscar forced a smile. "I've changed my mind. I had a late lunch, so I'm really not hungry."

"Not a problem at all."

"Where can I get a good cup of coffee?"

She gestured to his left and smiled. "Try The Sweet Tooth Cafe. They feature coffee from all over the world and offer delectable, mouth-watering desserts."

The woman sounded like a radio commercial.

Oscar smiled. "Thank you."

She smiled. "Thank *you*."

He arrived at The Sweet Tooth Cafe and peeked inside. The walls were decorated with pictures of various desserts and coffee beans. It was a small, well-lit place. Quiet. Maybe only thirty or forty people were inside. The aroma drew him in.

He ordered a double-shot latte and scooted off to the side. A few minutes later, the barista called his name and he grabbed his drink. After he added some sugar, he placed the cup on one of the empty tables and headed to the dessert display.

A tall woman stood in front of the desserts by herself,

obviously contemplating the various choices. She was pretty, but in a simple way. Not a lot of makeup or jewelry. Few women had the confidence to sport a short strawberry-blonde hairdo like she did and she wore it well. She looked fantastic in her lavender top, but it didn't appear that she dressed to impress like so many other women he'd met. He liked that. She continued to inspect the desserts, deep in thought.

There were cupcakes with pink frosting. Chocolate mousse. Tiramisu. Fruit tarts. And one chocolate eclair on the center platter all by itself. They must be good if there was only one left. His decision was easy, but the woman looked perplexed.

Oscar grabbed a plate and pointed to the desserts. "Difficult for you to choose?"

She glanced over at him with her lovely hazel eyes and flinched, obviously recognizing him. "Too many choices . . ." She returned her attention back to the table.

"Sometimes it's better not to think so much," he said, reaching for the last chocolate eclair. To his surprise she reached at the same time and they bumped hands.

They both dropped their arms back down to their sides and turned toward each other. They exchanged mutual keep-your-grimy-hands-off-my-dessert looks hidden behind toothy smiles. Then they both reached again for the eclair, bumping hands for the second time.

Oscar pointed to the eclair. "I believe this dessert is mine."

"Why would you think that?"

"It's simple. You've been standing here for a while, obviously. Undecided. You even said there were lots of choices."

"I didn't say they were *good* choices."

"Your empty plate means you were considering more than one of them. For me, there was never any doubt which dessert I wanted, so it would make sense for you to let me have it. Your eyes are very sweet and I have a feeling you'll do the right thing. You can grab one of the others that you had already considered a good possibility."

She nodded as if she had bought his bull. "You said that with one breath. I'm impressed."

"Thank you, I try."

"Of course that's only possible when you're full of hot air."

"Touché." He grinned and reached for the eclair again.

She slapped the top of his hand before he could grab it. "Leave it."

Oscar blinked. "You're talking to me as if I were a dog."

"If the leash fits . . ."

Oscar laughed and admired the confident woman who had just hit and insulted him. He was okay with that. There was something in her eyes that told him she was only half-serious. She glared at him, almost looking as if she dared him to make another move.

He reached for the eclair again.

"Wait a minute," she said. "I'm thinking."

"Do you need help?"

"No."

He was impressed with this fascinating and beautiful stranger, but there was no way in hell she would get that eclair.

Oscar grinned. "Your minute is up. My move." He snagged the eclair and stuck it on his plate. "Check."

Before he could blink the woman reached over, plucked the eclair from his plate and placed it on her own plate.

She smirked. "Checkmate." Then she turned and walked away.

Sydney held the laughter in as she grabbed a napkin from the dispenser on the counter and headed back to her table. She had just fought with Oscar Martin over an eclair. What had come over her? It was just an eclair! Still, she loved the surprised look on his face when she'd smacked his hand. And when she stole the eclair from his plate.

Of course, she knew all about Oscar. Women had gone gaga over his amazing, deep brown Spanish eyes and well-conditioned chestnut hair when he appeared on *Ellen*. He looked a hundred times more amazing in person than he did on television. It was obvious Silicon Valley's most eligible bachelor was used to getting what he wanted.

Too bad he wouldn't get it from her.

She arrived at her table where Gina sipped her chai tea latte. Gina's eyes grew wide.

Sydney turned around and jumped back when she saw

AN ECLAIR TO REMEMBER

Oscar, almost losing the eclair on her plate. "You look like a lost puppy."

Oscar blinked. "Another dog reference." He cocked his head to the side and grinned. "Who are you?"

"Sydney St. James. Eclair eater."

He eyed the diamond engagement ring on her finger and nodded. "You're something, Miss St. James. My name is—"

"Oscar Martin!" Gina jumped up and held out her hand close to his mouth. "Of course we know who you are. I'm Gina Strafford, pleased to meet you."

Oscar chuckled and kissed her hand. "Nice to meet you as well, although I do have an issue with your friend. She stole my eclair."

Gina gasped. "I can't believe you did that, Sydney." Gina reached over, grabbed the eclair from Sydney's plate and slapped it on Oscar's. "There you go. So sorry."

"Hey! Give me that." Sydney grabbed the eclair back and put it on her plate. She glared at Oscar. "And what are you doing talking with us? You're engaged."

He eyed her engagement ring. "Just like you, I can see." He glanced at the eclair on her plate. "What does my engagement have to do with me wanting that eclair?"

She pulled it back out of reach in case he tried to make a move for it. "You tell me."

A sexy grin appeared on his face. "Are you trying to confuse me?"

"Are you confused?"

"Maybe I am. Maybe I'm not."

Gina threw up her hand. "I'm confused."

Oscar scratched the side of his face. "You won't feel guilty eating that eclair knowing how much I wanted it?"

Sydney shook her head. "Not at all."

He looked over her shoulder and squinted. "No problem. I can see there are more eclairs on the way. Bigger ones. And probably fresher than the one you have." He pointed to her eclair and wrinkled his nose. "That looks like it might be a day old."

Sydney turned to look behind her but nobody was there. She knew she fell for his ruse when she felt pressure on her plate and turned back around.

Her eclair was gone and Oscar was lifting it toward his mouth.

"Wait!" she said, a little too loudly. Just about every head in the cafe turned in their direction.

The eclair was inches from his mouth. "Yes?"

She had to think of something quick. She didn't want him to win.

She held out her plate. "Give me the eclair."

He stared at her plate for a moment and grinned. "No." Then he took a bite.

"Stop!" She lunged forward and tried to grab the eclair but instead jammed it into his face.

She stepped back and threw a hand over her mouth.

Oscar stopped chewing. "You think this is funny . . . not a surprise. Odd, I find it difficult to breathe and chew at the same time. Must be because I have some of this delectable, mouth-watering dessert inside of my nose." He ran a finger across his frosting-covered cheek and stuck it in his mouth. "This is a wonderful eclair. Too bad you didn't get one. Anyway, I'll go get cleaned up."

"You do that."

He took a step toward the restroom and stopped. "Just one more thing . . ."

Sydney sighed. "What now?"

He licked his finger again. "Do you believe in love at first fight?"

CHAPTER THREE

The next day the ship was at sea and Oscar spent most of the time reading on the balcony. He ordered room service for both breakfast and lunch, but planned on attending dinner in the main dining room tonight. Leo had arranged for him to eat at the captain's table. Being in control of one of the largest vessels in the world was something Oscar admired, but he was more fascinated by the fact that the captain was an American woman. There were only two female American cruise ship captains in the entire world and he looked forward to the honor of chatting with one of them.

Speaking of admiration, Oscar couldn't get his mind off of the lovely Miss St. James.

He had enjoyed the little game they played last night with the eclair, even if it didn't end the way he had hoped. For her it wasn't really about wanting to eat the eclair. She just didn't want *him* to have it. It was about winning. She was aware that he usually got what he wanted and she wanted to prove a point.

You can't have everything.

She obviously knew about his reputation with the ladies from the tabloids, but she didn't know the tabloids got it wrong most of the time. She didn't know that the more he was in the news and the tabloids, the more exposure his company got. Publicity equaled money. That's why the cruise company had no problem giving Oscar a suite that would normally cost someone three thousand dollars a night.

He liked Sydney St. James. She was different. It was obvious she didn't want to be like other women.

And she wasn't. Not even close.

He wondered to whom Sydney was engaged and why her fiancé wasn't with her. Engaged or not engaged, he wanted to know more about her.

The doorbell rang and Oscar flew down the stairs from the loft in his suite toward the entryway. Leo had said he would stop by in the late afternoon after he hosted The Newlywed Game in the McKinley Showroom.

He opened the door and Leo walked right by him. "Only have a few minutes. Let's talk on the balcony."

"Okay." Oscar followed his friend to the balcony and sat on the lounge chair next to him. It was a beautiful day on the ocean and he assumed they were somewhere off the coast of Oregon. But Leo wasn't there to talk about GPS coordinates. "What's up?"

"Be careful."

Oscar turned to Leo and squished his eyebrows together. "What are we talking about here? Falling overboard?"

"Eclairs."

"Ahh . . . How did you know? Never mind. I forgot you know everything."

"I do. And remember we have the press on board. *New York Times. Wall Street Journal.* Radio. Television. Travel magazines. Blogs. You name it, they're here. They were told to respect your privacy and just stick to stories about our inaugural cruise but there's no guarantee. And what are you doing flirting with engaged women?"

"I wasn't flirting. We just had a brief conversation on how to choose a dessert."

Leo nodded. "A conversation that ended with an eclair in your face?"

"Give my compliments to the pastry chef. The ten percent that actually made it into my mouth was fantastic." Oscar grinned. "Hey, do me a favor."

"I know that look on your face and the answer is no."

"Make sure Sydney St. James and her friend are at the captain's table tonight."

Leo waved his finger at Oscar. "No, no, no. Not a good idea."

"Make it happen."

"The seats have been assigned. The only opening is Alexa's seat."

"It needs to be both of them. She'll say no if her friend isn't invited, too."

"I would have to move two people to another night. No way."

"How do you think the general public would feel if they read that Oscar Martin, the second sexiest man alive, disliked this cruise and became gravely ill on the food?"

"Nice try. You don't have a cruel bone in your body."

Oscar thought about it for a moment. "Okay, how about this one: In one of my interviews I'll say this was one of the best vacations of my life and I can't wait to do it again. I'll also highly recommend everyone putting this cruise on their bucket list."

Leo jumped up from the lounge chair. "I'll process your request immediately."

"Good." He grinned. "I like the customer service here. It's impressive."

Leo rolled his eyes. "I have a bad feeling about this."

"That's odd, because I feel fantastic."

Sydney and Gina were escorted through the dining room to the captain's table. There must have been a thousand people for this seating. The majority of the men wore sports jackets and ties. Most of the women, including Sydney and Gina, wore cocktail dresses of various styles and lengths, some silk, some rayon, some beaded. Sydney was most comfortable in jeans when she wasn't working.

She grimaced but continued to walk. "My feet are killing me."

Gina laughed. "You've only been walking five minutes. Suck it up, because all of the looks you're getting make it totally worth it."

"They're looking at you."

Gina squeezed Sydney's arm. "You're so good for my ego."

The invitation was last minute and a complete surprise, but the cruise director had said they often picked random guests to dine with the captain. No way Sydney could pass that up. What a way to spend the second night on the ship.

Of course, the first night hadn't been so bad either. Who would have thought she would meet Oscar Martin in person? Smashing an eclair in his face was a treat and also payback for all the hearts he'd ever broken, though she did have a tiny bit of guilt afterward. She had spent most of the day in her cabin to avoid seeing the man. And she knew there was no chance of seeing him for dinner since most likely he would eat at one of the specialty restaurants that were considered upgrades. Better that way. She was an engaged woman and needed to act like one. No more fun with the sexy Spaniard.

They arrived at their table and the captain stood, extending her hand. "I'm Captain Helen Duhart. Welcome."

Sydney accepted her hand. "Sydney St. James. Thank you for the honor."

Introductions were made all around the table and the two of them took a seat at the opposite end of the table from the captain next to a retired couple, Andy and Alice Anderson.

Andy perked up in his chair. "You can call us Triple A!"

Alice patted his hand. "Settle down, dear. You'll scare them."

He ignored his wife and turned to Sydney. "You know where we're from?"

Sydney shook her head. "I don't."

"Bummerville, California. It's really a city. Look it up! Ain't that a bummer? Ha!"

His ears wiggled when he laughed.

It was a privilege to sit at the captain's table, but Sydney had a feeling she would soon be annoyed with the man sitting next to her. She wouldn't mind making a move to the empty seat next to the captain, but that would be cruel to leave Gina there with Mr. Bummer.

A few minutes later, the captain stood again and shook hands with Oscar Martin.

Gina tapped the side of her leg. "Well, would you look at that . . ."

Oh, she'd looked, all right. She didn't think the man could get any more good looking, but that tailored black suit kicked his sexiness up a notch.

Introductions were made around the table again and Oscar sat. He turned and locked eyes with Sydney, giving her a wink and smile.

Gina leaned sideways toward Sydney. "I want him to

look at *me* that way. What are you doing to get that reaction out of him?"

"I'm not doing anything!" she whispered. "I'm just sitting here."

"Well, I need to learn to sit like you."

The waiters arrived and placed the salads on the table as Sydney pulled a piece of bread from the basket and placed it on her plate.

"Welcome, ladies and gentlemen!" said the booming voice from the overhead speakers. Leo Grant appeared next to their table with a cordless microphone and a spotlight shining on him.

Gina tapped Sydney on the side of her leg. "Holy moly, this guy is gorgeous, too."

Sydney turned to Gina. "Are you ovulating or something? That's the cruise director, the one who invited us."

Gina smiled at the man. "Remind me to thank him later."

"I'm your cruise director, Leo Grant. Welcome! Our fabulous chefs have prepared an amazing meal for you this evening and we hope you enjoy it. As always, please let us know if there is anything we can do to make your cruising experience even better. And I would now like to pass the microphone over to someone special. Please . . . a warm round of applause for Captain Helen Duhart!"

The room filled with applause and cheers as Captain Helen stood and took the microphone from the cruise director.

She waved and smiled. "Thank you. I know I had the pleasure of meeting many of you last night at the welcome reception, but I wanted to take a moment to say welcome to those who were not there. This will be a trip of a lifetime and it's a pleasure to take you to one of the most beautiful and pristine parts of the world. Please come say hello during dinner. Enjoy your meal!"

She handed the microphone back to the cruise director as the passengers applauded.

Gina leaned forward and smiled. "Captain Helen, how did you get started doing this? Is there a captain school or something?"

"Ha!" said Andy. "Captain school. Good one."

Captain Helen smiled. "I got my business administration degree from California Maritime Academy as well as a third-mate unlimited U.S. Coast Guard license. That allows me to sail anything I want, from a tugboat to the largest cruise ship in the world. And anything in between."

Oscar stood and gestured to Gina. "Please, Miss Strafford. Take my seat so you can speak comfortably with the captain."

That was rather kind of the Spaniard to offer the best seat in the house to her best friend. On second thought, if Gina moved, then Oscar would be seated next to her. Wow. This guy was smooth. She had to think of something quickly.

Sydney stood. "I'd like to speak with the captain as well." She glanced down at Gina. "Can I go first?" She angled her head so only Gina could see her face and whispered, "Say yes."

"Of course!" Gina practically screamed. Not great acting, but it worked.

Oscar hesitantly pulled his chair out and waved Sydney over. As she sat, he leaned in close to her ear. "Are you scared of me?"

The heat from his breath sent chills across Sydney's body. "Uh . . . not at all."

"Are you familiar with serendipity?" he whispered. "Because I think this would qualify. Out of all the tables here we ended up at the same one."

Serendipity. Right. Like she believed in that stuff.

Oscar moved around the table and joined her best friend. He sat and winked at Sydney, then turned his attention to Gina.

The captain smiled at Sydney. "How was your first twenty-four hours on board?"

Sydney pried her eyes off Oscar and turned to Captain Helen. "Wonderful. This ship is amazing."

Over the next ten minutes or so, Sydney talked with the captain and found it very difficult not to look across the table at Oscar. Now she was getting restless and curious. Oscar and Gina seemed to be having a lively conversation.

The room was getting louder and she couldn't hear a thing over the noise except when Gina laughed. Gina glanced over at Sydney and waved. This wasn't fair. They were having so much fun.

Captain Helen leaned closer. "Looks like tomorrow

will be another beautiful day at sea. Sunny and in the mid-seventies."

"We really lucked out with the weather." Sydney popped out of her chair. "Excuse me, Captain Helen."

"Of course."

Sydney worked her way back around the table, Oscar's eyes on her the entire time.

He stood as she approached. "Welcome back, Miss St. James. Would you like your seat back?"

Sydney shook her head. "No, thank you. Gina, would you please accompany me to the ladies' room? I'd like to freshen up."

Oscar took a half step closer to Sydney. "You're wasting your time."

Sydney crossed her arms. "What are you talking about?"

"This freshening up you want to do . . . It would be an impossibility for you to be more fresh and vibrant and lovely than you already are at this moment."

Sydney uncrossed her arms. Her legs got weak. "Gina? Please . . ."

Gina's eyes shifted to Oscar and then returned to Sydney. "Well, she may not need freshening up, but I certainly do. Excuse us, Oscar."

"By all means . . ."

Sydney avoided eye contact with Oscar. She and Gina both grabbed their purses, locked arms, and walked toward the restroom.

Gina giggled. "This is so much fun. And that man is—"

"Engaged."

"True. You think it's a marriage of convenience? Maybe the guy needs a green card in a hurry or something."

Sydney pushed the bathroom door open. "He's a US citizen."

They approached the sink and Sydney stared at herself in the mirror.

What was going on? That man was getting Sydney all flustered.

Gina rubbed Sydney's back. "What's going on, sweetie? Why the big escape?"

Sydney turned on the faucet and let the water run over her fingers. "Oscar is . . ."

"Delicious?"

Sydney turned to Gina and gave her a look. "You're not helping."

"How can you not think he's gorgeous? Let me check your pulse because that man is flirting with you."

"I don't care. And if you're asking me whether I think the guy is attractive or not, the answer is yes. Of course. Someone in a coma could see that, but that's not my point. He's engaged. I'm engaged. And I need you to do me a favor."

"Anything."

"Be my shield. You need to protect me."

Gina laughed. "Protect you from what?"

"Temptation."

Oscar glanced toward the restrooms again for Sydney and Gina. He wondered how much freshening up a woman could do. He doubted he had scared her away, but what was taking them so long? Their salads were sitting there untouched and the main courses would be coming out soon.

He'd been serious when he'd told her she needed nothing at all. That woman was perfection from head to toe. It bothered him a little that she hadn't responded to him like other women had. He'd seen glimpses of something in her eyes when they were close to each other —a spark. Still, she kept her cool under pressure. He liked that.

Sure, she was engaged but he wasn't convinced she was madly in love with the guy, whoever he was. If Sydney were Oscar's fiancée he wouldn't be able to stand that much time apart from her. Of course Alexa had let him go, so what did that say about his own fiancée and their relationship?

"Oscar!"

He'd only met her once but he had memorized her voice. He turned and smiled. "Hello, Joanne. Where's Raymond?"

"Oh, he's taking a nap." She sat in Gina's chair. "You ever been out with an older woman?"

Oscar studied her for a moment. "Can't say that I have. How old are you, Joanne?"

She waved her finger at him. "You know it's not polite to ask a woman that."

He grabbed her hand and her eyes grew wider. "How young are you?"

"Seventy-two," she blurted out.

"Own it. Don't be ashamed of how old you are. You know it's just a number, right?" She nodded. "Good. On paper you're seventy-two but in your heart you're still forty."

Joanne smiled. "Thirty."

"Very good!" He pulled her hand to his mouth and kissed it. "You don't need to find someone younger or have an affair. I'll give you some advice after dinner. A few things you can do to spice up your relationship and wake up the passion hiding inside of your husband."

"You're the best, Oscar. Thank you."

As Joanne walked away, Sydney approached with Gina.

Oscar stood. "Welcome back."

She avoided eye contact with him. "Thank you. I'll take my seat back now. It looks like they're starting to serve dinner."

Oscar glanced around the room and could see the waiters arriving with food. "Of course." He pulled the chair out for her and she sat. He returned to his chair next to the captain without another word. He watched Sydney as she ate her salad.

The dinner was fantastic—not a surprise considering it was a luxury cruise. Oscar enjoyed the lasagna and he saw that Sydney did as well. The staff came around to clear the plates and a few minutes after that they brought out the dessert. Crème brûlée.

As the waiter placed the dessert in front of him, Oscar winked at Sydney. She quickly looked away.

Oscar turned to the captain. "I believe Miss Strafford would still like to speak with you. Do you mind if I change places with her?"

"Not at all."

"Great. One moment." Oscar stood and grabbed his crème brûlée and spoon. He made his way over to Sydney and Gina. "Excuse me, Miss Strafford. You can speak with the captain now. Please take my seat."

She lit up. "Really? I'd love that."

Oscar pointed to her dish. "Take your dessert with you."

"Right! Good idea." Gina walked over and sat next to the captain.

Oscar took Gina's seat but didn't speak. He took a spoonful of the crème brûlée into his mouth and moaned. "This is wonderful." He glanced over at Sydney. "Although I still prefer the eclair from last night. I especially loved how it was served. With a fist."

Sydney threw her hand over her mouth, which was a shame. Her smile was like sunshine. But that was a good sign. She wasn't completely shut down.

"I must say, Miss St. James . . . May I call you Sydney?"

"No."

"Very well. I'll call you Sunshine because of the way you light up the room."

"Did that line work on your fiancée?"

"Truthfully, I have never said that to anyone before in my life. I see you have an issue with me having a fiancée. I don't have an issue with yours."

She pushed her empty dessert dish away. "You and I aren't going to happen. I know your type. You can charm fish out of the water."

He grinned. "So, you think I'm charming?"

"I'm saying I saw you coming from a mile away and you're a modern day Don Juan."

He leaned in closer to her. "The only thing Don Juan and I have in common is our Spanish names. I admit I'm drawn to you. It's crazy, I know. I also admit there is this tiny little problem of both of us being engaged."

"It really is no problem since nothing will happen between us."

He made a big display out of licking his spoon, front and back. "Don't be too sure."

CHAPTER FOUR

The next morning Sydney stared through the porthole of their tiny cabin. She and Gina had eaten breakfast and were getting ready to head to the indoor pool for a little swim to work off the calories. No way she'd allow herself to put on weight considering she had a wedding dress to fit into. She had slept well after a rough start. How can a woman fall asleep with the voice and scent of Oscar Martin on her mind? Not easy. That man was going to drive her crazy.

Gina stretched to the floor and grabbed her toes. "Any orcas out there?"

"The porthole is fogged up. I can't see a thing."

"Then why are you looking out?"

"Uh . . ."

"Your mind is on the hunky man from Spain?"

Sydney flipped around and threw her hands in the air.

"I don't get why he's flirting with me. There are plenty of other women on the ship."

"His selection is limited since half the passengers traveling with us are over sixty-five. Plus, you look marvelous, darling."

They laughed as they slipped on their bathing suits. Gina was an amazing friend who had always been there for Sydney. They had met at the travel agency many years ago and Gina now planned events for a software company. She was happy because she still got to travel, unlike Sydney. They'd joked about working together again one day but she didn't see how that was possible when she worked so much as an admin. Still, you never know where life could take you and it's best to be open to other possibilities.

She was very open to it.

Ten minutes later, they went up to the top deck where the indoor pool and hot tubs were located. They walked through the steamy glass doors and could smell the chlorine from the pool. The smell made her smile. Her nickname in high school was Fish because she was always in the water. She was a member of the swimming team, the diving team, and the water polo team. She had always loved being by the water whether it was a pool, a lake, or an ocean. She had definitely been a fish in a previous life.

It almost seemed unreal they could have a pool that big on a ship. It was huge and she was excited to get in. And luckily there weren't too many people there. An older couple in one of the hot tubs, a few people reading in lounge chairs by the edge of the pool. And a man doing laps in lane one. She watched him for a moment and was impressed. He had good form, keeping his head down, even breaths, consistent strokes. Definitely an athlete.

Sydney pointed to a couple of empty chairs by the showers. "Let's leave our things over there."

"Sounds good."

They walked around to the other side of the pool and dropped their bags on the chairs. They slipped off their wraps and walked to the showers to rinse before entering the pool. Sydney slid under the rope to start swimming in the deep end. She dipped herself all the way under, enjoying the temperature of the water, the soothing feeling against her skin.

The lanes were two wide, meaning two people could swim at the same time. The only thing that was required was that they go in opposite directions and at almost the same speed so they wouldn't ram into each other.

Gina had never been much of a swimmer but she didn't mind being in the water, so she floated in the shallow end as Sydney started her laps. She needed a little bit of warmup and then she could really get going.

Time to burn off those pancakes.

After about twenty laps Sydney noticed she'd caught up with the man in her lane. She must have picked up speed after she warmed up. She slowed her pace, but then the guy swam even slower. Then he stopped in front of her.

She passed him underneath the water and eyed his

physique. He was in amazing shape. She came up for air, did a flip against the wall and kept moving. Hopefully, he'd be out of the water by the time she made it back his way. She didn't mind people being in the lanes with her but there was certain protocol you were supposed to follow. Keep moving. When she worked her way back to the other side the man had disappeared.

Better. More room.

She continued to swim and heard Gina's crazy laugh, but continued with her strokes. A lap later she heard her laugh again, and pulled up from the water to see what her best friend was up to. She wiped the water from her eyes and froze.

No way.

Gina was talking with Oscar. *He* had been the man swimming in her lane earlier and she hadn't even known it. She worked her way back under the rope to the shallow end and exited the pool using the stairs. His back was to her, so she couldn't help but take a quick glance at his butt. If only she had a camera.

Sydney wasn't watching where she was going and crammed her foot into a lounge chair, stubbing a few of her toes. "Ouch!" She reached down to grab her foot and slipped back, bumping a small table. The table scraped against the cement creating a loud screeching sound. She twisted to try to keep the table from bumping into the large man lounging in his Speedo. Instead, she lost her balance again and landed right in the man's lap.

The man smiled. "Hi. I'm Hank."

Oscar rushed over, a concerned look on his face. "Are you okay?"

"Yes."

The pain wasn't from the stubbed toes anymore. It was from embarrassment.

Oscar held out his hand. "Let me help you."

She stared at his hand and hesitated. Then she grabbed it.

He pulled her up so she was almost face-to-face with him. That's when she noticed he wasn't wearing a shirt. And why would he be? He had just finished swimming. She did her best to keep eye contact even though she wanted so much to drop her gaze to his chest. And his abs. But she knew exactly what they were like. Perfect. She had seen them as she was passing him underwater.

Oscar grinned. "This is serendipity. Again."

"We're on the same ship. That's *not* serendipity."

"It most certainly is."

Sydney shook her head. "If we were both on separate ships and they crashed into each other and you and I ended up on the same lifeboat—*maybe* that would be serendipity. But even then I would be wondering if you had paid the captain to crash your ship into my ship."

He chuckled. "I love the way your creative mind works. But I'll explain to you why this is serendipity. There are over four thousand people on this ship and only seven people at the pool. You and I are two of those people. What are the chances? Seven in four thousand. Serendipity."

She still didn't buy it. There must have been a way he had found out she was going to be there. But how? She and Gina had just made the decision to go to the pool earlier at breakfast.

"You look a little bit hazy." He pointed toward Gina. "Why don't we go and sit down?"

She used the opportunity to quickly glance down at his chest. It was perfection.

He grinned. "Do you like what you see?"

Some men shouldn't be that good-looking.

She dropped his hand and shrugged her shoulders. "I've seen better."

He chuckled. "I'm not surprised. A woman like you could have any man in the world."

She felt powerless around him and had to get away. She walked toward Gina without responding. The bathing suit she had picked out was flattering, but she wondered if he was watching her at that moment. He'd better not be.

Oscar admired Sydney as she walked over to her friend. He couldn't help but let his eyes travel down to Sydney's backside. No photo or painting would ever do that butt justice. It had to be seen and appreciated live in person to be able to take in the glory of it all. And it wasn't just that. Every part of her was perfect.

Sydney had wrapped the towel around her body just as he joined them.

He pointed to her toes. "You okay?"

"Fine. Thank you. Enjoy the rest of your day."

He nodded. "This is your nonchalant way of telling me to take a hike. I understand."

He turned to walk away and hoped he would only have to travel a few steps.

"Wait!" said Sydney, from behind him.

He removed the smile from his face and replaced it with his best frown. Then he turned around. "Yes?"

Sydney shrugged. "Sorry—that was rude."

He smiled and moved closer. "If it makes you feel any better you can smash an eclair in my face."

She laughed. "Not today. As long as you behave."

"Are you looking forward to Ketchikan tomorrow?" asked Gina.

Oscar nodded. "It's a wonderful little fisherman's village. Friendly people, places to shop and eat. You'll love it. Have lunch at Alaska Fish House and try the salmon fish and chips. Ketchikan is the salmon capital of the world so you know how good it has to be."

"Sounds yummy. When was the last time you were there?"

He grabbed his towel and wrapped it around his waist. "A little over ten years ago on another cruise. Coincidentally, it was the inaugural sailing for a different company and I documented part of the trip, shooting photos for their website and brochures."

How did the topic get to photos? That's not something

he had wanted to talk about. As much as he missed it, that part of his life was over.

Sydney slid into her sandals and glanced back at Oscar. "A travel photographer? You?"

"Yes. Don't looked so shocked."

"It's just . . . I think it would be a fun job."

"The best."

"You must be looking forward to taking photos on this cruise then."

He shrugged. "No photos this time."

"Oh. You forgot your camera?"

"No, that's not it. It's just . . . I don't know. We'll see. My photo-taking days were long ago." He forced a smile. "My life is different now."

Gina stuck her finger in her ear and shook it. "I know you're busy inventing cars that fly, but why did you give up the photography? Couldn't you do both?"

This conversation was definitely going in the wrong direction. "Long story. Not really worth talking about." He gestured to the door. "I'm heading back to my suite. If I don't see you later, enjoy yourselves and hopefully I'll see you tomorrow in Ketchikan."

"Okay, that was strange," said Sydney, walking with Gina back to their cabin. "I touched a nerve, didn't I? Did you see how quickly his mood changed?"

"Oh, yeah. Something's happening there. He's got some baggage."

"I didn't think he had a care in the world. It shocked me, actually. And now I'm curious and want to know more."

Gina pressed the button for the elevator. "Me, too."

"But did I say anything inappropriate?"

"No way! Don't worry about it. We were just chatting about the trip and photography. You were fine —believe me."

Sydney hoped so, but wondered why she cared if she'd hurt his feelings. It's not like they had a future together or were even friends. They were two people who happened to be vacationing on the same cruise together, that's all.

Sydney and Gina ordered room service and enjoyed a couple of Chinese chicken salads in their cabin.

Gina perked up. "Are you in the mood to check out the casino? Since you wouldn't let me take you to Vegas, I've been in the mood to gamble. Maybe a little blackjack . . ."

"That sounds like a great idea."

They got dressed and made their way up to the casino. Surprisingly many other passengers had the same idea. The casino was alive with action. Sydney scanned the room. There was blackjack, craps, slot machines. Many of the games you'd see in a typical Las Vegas casino.

The largest group of people gathered around one of the tables in the center of the room. People were screaming and high-fiving each other.

Sydney pointed in that direction. "What's going on over there?"

"I think it's roulette and someone must be winning. Let's check it out."

They walked past the twenty-five cent slots and made their way around to the opening behind the glass on the back of the roulette wheel.

Then Sydney froze.

Oscar's voice popped back into her head.

Serendipity.

Okay, she never mentioned to anyone she was going to go to the casino. And Oscar never mentioned anything, either.

But there was the Spanish man, smiling and having a great time with a large group of onlookers. She glanced down at the table and he had a huge stack of his chips on the color red. The dealer had just matched his stack, but he didn't pull his winnings.

"Let it ride again!" said Oscar.

The onlookers cheered as the dealer picked up the small white ball and let it spin around the wheel.

Gina pointed at his bet. "Look at that stack of chips."

"I'm looking . . ."

As if he knew he was being watched, Oscar glanced over and winked at Sydney. The ball slowed down and was almost ready to drop, but he didn't seem to care. He kept eye contact with Sydney as the dealer yelled, "Twenty-five! Red!"

More screams and high-fives were exchanged around

the table as the dealer matched Oscar's stack of chips. Then she swapped out the smaller chips for larger ones.

"How much does he have there?" asked Gina.

"I don't know. I think the black chips are a hundred each."

"He must have fifteen or twenty of them there. Do you think he'll bet it again?"

"Hopefully not. If he knows anything about odds his luck is about to run out."

"Let it ride on red!" yelled Oscar.

The man was crazy.

More people gathered around and they were now cheering his name, "Oscar! Oscar! Oscar!"

Gina grabbed Sydney's arm. "Come on, I need to be closer for this one."

They squeezed through a few people and scooted up right next to Oscar.

He smiled. "Welcome ladies." He held up his index finger to the dealer. "One moment." The dealer waited for Oscar and he turned to Sydney. "Care to join the fun?"

Sydney shook her head. "No way. I'll just watch. How many times in a row have you won on red?"

He smiled. "Six."

"Are you insane? No way it'll be red again. The odds must be a gazillion to one. You've been lucky, but you may want to change it to black. It's time."

"Do you think so? My gut still tells me it's red so I wanted to do it one more time."

She grimaced. "I'll look away because I don't want to see that giant stack of yours disappear."

The dealer gestured to Oscar. "All ready?"

"Hold on." He stared at Sydney for a moment, obviously contemplating what she had said. Then he turned toward the dealer. "I've changed my mind." He reached over the table and slid the entire stack of chips over to black. "There. Let's do this."

"Okay!" said the dealer, sliding the ball into the groove and whipping it around the wheel. "No more bets!"

Sydney's heart rate accelerated as she watched the white ball spin around the roulette wheel. She was so glad Oscar changed it. That would have been crazy leaving it on red again.

But something horrible just crossed her mind.

What if the ball doesn't land on black? It had better be black.

People screamed for black. The energy in the room was electric. Sydney didn't want to look like a fool and needed to summon the energy of the luck gods, so she began to cheer along with the guests. "Black! Black! Black!"

The ball slowed down, just about to drop. It bounced off the edge of the black eight and jumped back on to the rail for a brief moment before settling into the slot below.

"Fourteen!" yelled the dealer. "Red!"

And just like that, the excitement at the table faded. Every head at the table turned in her direction.

A man pointed to Sydney. "You shouldn't have

listened to her. You were on fire until she came along." He slapped Oscar on the back and walked away.

"That can't be," mumbled Sydney.

She stared at the roulette wheel. The dumb white ball sat in the dumb fourteen-red slot. Her eyes started to burn. She watched as the dealer leaned over the table and took away Oscar's winnings.

Every single chip. Gone.

CHAPTER FIVE

Oscar sat on the balcony and stared out at Ketchikan, the most southeastern city in Alaska. Known as the rain capital of the state, it was located seven hundred miles north of Seattle, Washington. Today there would be no rain in sight. It was sunny and warm. A jacket wouldn't even be necessary.

Many of the passengers had disembarked and were making their way in and out of the seasonal shops on Front Street. The stop today would be the shortest of all the ports during the cruise—long enough for Oscar to go for a nice walk, peek in a store or two, and get some fish and chips at Alaska Fish House.

At the moment he was trying to sort out his thoughts and come up with a plan for when he returned to San Francisco. He hated the thought of hurting Alexa, but he needed to call off the wedding the moment he got back. They wouldn't be happy together. His only regret was not doing it earlier. He had hoped the cruise would bring them back closer together again but obviously, that plan had failed.

He also needed to analyze his professional life and really decide which direction he wanted to go next. He'd had success but wasn't fulfilled, and that needed to change.

One thing was for sure, being in touch with nature tended to open up a person and give him clarity. Coming on this cruise had been a great idea. He looked forward to experiencing the grandeur around him that a person could easily take for granted.

Speaking of beauty . . .

His thoughts turned back to Sydney.

Being in the presence of that attractive, feisty woman was like a shot of adrenaline and he looked forward to seeing her again. He felt bad for her yesterday, though. He was sure the ball would stop on red again at the roulette wheel but he changed it to black for her. What he hadn't expected was for her to cry. He had told her not to worry about it; it was just money. But she had mumbled, "I'm so sorry" and rushed off with Gina.

Hopefully she felt better today.

Oscar stood and looked past the office of tourism. A woman with short strawberry-blonde hair walked with another woman.

Sydney.

She was entering the Tongass Trading Company. He headed back inside the suite to change his clothes. All of a sudden he was in the mood for a walk.

Ten minutes later, Oscar entered the Tongass Trading Company and casually looked around. The place was packed with tourists from the ship. Sydney should be easy to spot since she was taller than most women.

And more beautiful.

The store had a variety of things for the traveler: footwear, outdoor wear, souvenirs, snacks. He made his way around the hiking boots and stopped at the beanies and hats. That's when he spotted Sydney by the table of Ketchikan sweatshirts. She was dressed casually, black jeans that fit her body to perfection and a solid turquoise blouse. She grabbed one of the sweatshirts and held it against her body as her friend Gina nodded her approval. Then Sydney turned and spotted him.

He quickly plucked a fishing hat from the rack and slapped it on top of his head. Sydney tapped Gina on the arm and they both walked in his direction.

He forced a smile, hoping they didn't think he followed them. "Good morning, ladies. Beautiful day. I hope you're doing better this morning, Sunshine."

"Don't call me that." Sydney held out her hand. "Can I see that hat?"

He stared at her hand for a moment. "Why?"

"I'll tell you in a second."

It was odd that she wanted to look at it, but he slid the hat off of his head and handed it to her.

"Thank you." She turned and walked away.

Oscar watched as she walked to the other side of the store. What was she up to?

Gina waved it off. "Just go with it. She's a little bit kooky this morning."

"Okay . . ."

"Besides the fish and chips, is there anything else you recommend while we're here?"

"Unfortunately, there isn't much time to go sightseeing. But there will be plenty of time for that when we get to Juneau in a couple of days."

She frowned. "Oh . . ."

"Ketchikan does have the world's largest collection of totem poles. They're scattered around the city and in some of the parks. Lots of tourists take pictures with them."

She smiled. "I'll look out for them."

Oscar looked over Gina's shoulder again. It almost felt like she was trying to distract him. What was Sydney doing? He was about to find out.

Sydney returned and handed Oscar a bag. "Merry Christmas."

"It's July."

"Merry July."

He hesitated but then took the bag from her, looking inside. The ridiculous hat he'd thrown on his head was inside. Also inside the bag were five boxes of breath mints and some dental floss.

He glanced up from the bag. "What are you trying to say?"

She shrugged. "Impulse shopping."

"I appreciate the gesture but you don't have to buy me gifts."

"Yes. I do."

He turned to Gina, hoping for an explanation.

She shrugged. "She came up with the idea of buying things for you every day until the end of the cruise. You know . . . to make up for what happened in the casino."

Oscar laughed. "That's not necessary."

Sydney's eyes looked a little moist. "Yes, it is."

His laugh faded. He didn't like that look on her face. Oh no. Was she going to cry again?

Sydney broke eye contact with Oscar and shifted her weight from one leg to the other. If another tear fell from her eyes she would hurl herself into the ocean as soon as she got back on the ship.

"Sydney, look at me."

She ignored Oscar and grabbed a snow globe from the table display. "These are nice. You want three or four of them?"

"Sydney, what happened in the casino was no big deal. It's just money. There are far more important things in life. Think of it this way, I only started with twenty dollars at the roulette wheel. So really, I lost just twenty dollars. The rest of the money wasn't even mine!"

"It was yours because you had won it and I helped you lose it." She reached behind him and snagged a polar bear shot glass. "I think you'd love one of these."

"No."

She frowned and set the shot glass back down. Her eyes grew wide as she picked up a box. "Look! Family packs!"

He grabbed the box from her and stuck it back in its place. "I don't need a family pack of polar bear shot glasses. And you can't go around buying me things the entire trip."

"Watch me."

He studied her for a few moments and grinned. "Fine. I guess that means we'll be spending more time together."

Sydney blinked.

She hadn't thought of that part.

Still, she felt horrible and wouldn't stray from the plan. She needed to be strong and resist his charming ways. It wouldn't be easy, considering the way he looked this morning. Hot. Even casually dressed in those jeans and white polo shirt he looked absolutely amazing.

Oscar waved Sydney toward the door and walked in that direction. "Come on, let's go shopping."

She and Gina followed him toward the door. Gina pointed to his firm butt and Sydney slapped her hand. "You don't have to point. I probably saw it before you."

Once outside, Oscar made a left on Front Street and walked along the sidewalk, occasionally looking back and smiling.

"This is no way to spend a vacation," said Gina. "There's a good chance I'll bail on you at some point."

"Don't you dare. You said you'd protect me."

Oscar stopped in front of Sweet Mermaids, a coffee and pastry shop. He glanced in the window and pointed.

"They have eclairs here. If you buy me eight hundred of them we should be even. But we may miss the ship's departure. How long does it take to smash eight hundred eclairs into someone's face?" He laughed and continued down the street.

Sydney let a loud breath. "Don't tempt me!"

Gina laughed and smacked her on the arm. "You asked for it." She grabbed Sydney by the hand and stopped. "Hey, Oscar. You hungry yet?"

"What are you doing?" whispered Sydney. "I don't want to eat with him."

He stopped and checked his watch. "I could eat. In fact, if we went now we'd beat most of the lunch crowd. Great idea, follow me." He turned around and headed in the opposite direction. He winked at Sydney and then flew past her. "My treat."

"No! It's not!" Sydney grabbed Gina's arm and pulled her in Oscar's direction. "I'm paying!"

Oscar laughed and picked up the pace. A few seconds later, Sydney passed him and felt more in control. She'd get to the restaurant first and give the waiter her credit card in advance, telling him she would pay and to not accept Oscar's credit card, no matter what he said or did. She'd even offer him a larger tip to make sure it happened.

Sydney took a few more steps and then stopped and shook her head. She was an idiot. She realized she was walking—almost running!—but had no idea where the restaurant was. She stopped and turned around. Gina and

Oscar were five buildings back, sitting at the bus stop. They laughed and pointed at her.

She placed her hands on her hips. "This is not funny! Lead the way and remember I'm paying!"

A couple of minutes later, they arrived at Alaska Fish House. Oscar was right; there weren't a lot of people there since it was early. There was only one problem. The place had no waiters. They were supposed to order and pay at the counter. She needed to come up with a different plan. The only thing she could do was make sure she was the last one to place an order so she would be standing directly in front of the cashier.

Oscar gestured toward the cashier. "Ladies first."

Sydney huffed. "You think you're so smooth."

Gina stepped forward and ordered the salmon fish and chips with a beer.

The cashier tapped her order into the computer and then looked up. "Got it. Next?"

Oscar smiled at Sydney. "Please . . ."

She shook her head and eyed the menu above their heads on the wall. "I'm not sure I know what I want yet. Go ahead."

Oscar winked at her and took a couple of steps toward the register. "I'll have the same."

"Two salmon fish and chips and two beers," said the cashier.

"Why not?" said Sydney. "I'll have the same."

As the cashier tapped Sydney's order into the computer, Oscar slid past Gina and used his hip to bump

Sydney out of the way. He handed the cashier his credit card and smiled. "Here you go."

Sydney slid right back and jammed her hip into his as hard as she could, knocking him into the long row of plastic ketchup bottles on the counter. Oscar grabbed the edge of the counter for stability but couldn't hang on and slammed to the floor, landing on top of fifteen to twenty ketchup bottles. Ketchup exploded in several directions, splattering the walls, the floor, as well as the legs and feet of some of the people waiting for their orders.

The restaurant turned silent as Sydney stood there in horror.

Oscar slowly got back up and turned in her direction with a *you've done it again* grin on his face.

She eyed his white polo shirt, now completely covered in ketchup. He even had some on his jeans and shoes. A woman and her teenage son grabbed some napkins from the dispenser on the counter and they wiped off their shoes. The woman didn't say anything but did glance up at Sydney for a moment to give her a look.

Sydney grimaced. "I'm sorry." She handed the cashier her credit card, even though she felt like she hadn't won. Now she needed to buy Oscar new clothes.

Oscar licked ketchup off his finger and chuckled. "You can't be trusted around food—that's for sure."

At least he didn't appear to be mad. How could he not be?

"I'm sorry," she repeated. Even after the second time of

saying the words it didn't seem like they were able to help repair any of the damage.

He glanced down at his polo shirt. "Really. It's no problem at all. As you well know, I'm a big fan of the color red."

Sydney felt her eyes begin to burn.

Oscar pointed to her face. "No, no, no. Please don't cry again. Don't do that."

Too late.

CHAPTER SIX

Later that evening Oscar walked across the promenade deck where all the entertainment and clubs were located. He headed to the Polar Lounge where Leo had said he would be hosting a question and answer session for the passengers. In two days they would have their first major stop on the cruise in Juneau and there were always questions about the excursions, sightseeing, and transportation around the city. Oscar didn't have any questions—he just wanted to watch his best friend in action and support him. He'd heard him make the morning announcements and saw his brief intro at the captain's dinner but he wanted to see more. Leo had told him he was having the time of his life and Oscar couldn't have been happier for him.

He checked his watch and realized the session had started a while ago. Hopefully, he'd be able to catch the end of it.

He entered the lounge and stood against the back wall. A man asked Leo how much smoked salmon he could bring back onboard the ship.

Leo grinned. "You can bring back as much as you want as long as you have enough to share with the crew." The guests laughed but then he took the time to give the man a serious answer before wrapping it up. "Thanks for stopping by. Don't forget the bar will remain open! Have a great evening."

The guests applauded and some headed for the exit while others went back to the bar for another drink.

At least Oscar had seen the last part of it. He shuffled through the people to the front and hugged Leo. "Great job, you're a natural. I caught the end."

"Thanks, man."

"You two know each other?" asked a female voice from behind.

Oscar turned around and smiled. "Hello, Gina. Yes, we know each other. Leo is my best friend."

Leo held out his hand. "Great meeting you, Gina."

Oscar looked over Gina's shoulder for Sydney but she wasn't in sight. Too bad.

"She'll be here soon," said Gina, reading his mind.

He smiled. "Good to hear."

Gina turned to Leo. "I never got a chance to say thank you for the invite to the captain's table on the second night. So . . . thank you."

"You're welcome. I need to head over to the disco to

make sure it's ready to go, but I can try to stop by later for a few minutes if you think you'll still be here."

"Oh . . ." Gina smiled. "Yeah, we plan on having a drink and relaxing here in the lounge for a little bit. Come back. Definitely."

"Great. See you later." He slapped Oscar on the back and winked.

Gina turned and watched him walk away. "He seems like a nice guy."

"He's the best."

"And what do you think of my friend Sydney?"

He grinned. "Direct questions—I like them. And I like Sydney. There's something special about her. I felt it the moment I met her. Could be the same feeling you're having right now."

"Me? What are you talking about?"

"My friend Leo. You like him."

Gina stared at Oscar for a moment and laughed. "You're good."

"I try."

"What do you try?" asked Sydney, approaching from behind.

Oscar turned and smiled. "I try to control myself when I'm in your presence because..." He glanced at her red dress. It was a little bit shorter than the black dress from the captain's dinner. He was never a big fan of kneecaps until today. "You look radiant. Lovely. Breath-taking."

She swallowed hard. "Uh . . . thank you."

"My pleasure."

They locked eyes for a few moments. A few glorious moments.

Gina cleared her throat. "Okay. I guess I'll stand here until you two are through."

Sydney stared at Gina like she spoke Chinese. "Huh?"

"Nothing. I'm thirsty. Drinks, anyone?"

"That sounds wonderful," said Oscar.

"My treat!" Sydney rushed to the bar.

Oscar laughed and followed Sydney and Gina to the bar. The night had taken a sudden turn in an unexpected direction and Oscar felt good about it. After the ketchup fiasco at Alaska Fish House, he thought Sydney would hide in her cabin for the rest of the cruise. Especially after she had cried again. What a great surprise to see her out and looking as lovely as ever.

Sydney tapped her fingers on the bar. "Do you have any two-thousand-dollar bottles of wine?"

Oscar stepped up, laughing. "Don't listen to her—she's drunk from the fumes in here. A glass of cabernet for me."

Sydney frowned. "You're no fun. Gin fizz for me."

Oscar scooted closer to Sydney. "I assure you I'm plenty of fun. And what is this gin fizz?"

"I don't know. It's kind of like a lemon Slurpee."

"Ahh. We have something like this in Spain, but without alcohol. It's called a Granizada. Refreshing on a hot summer's day. I changed my mind. I would like a gin fizz as well."

Sydney held her hand up for the bartender. "Two gin fizzes, please. Gina?"

"Martini."

They got their drinks and Gina pointed to an intimate place in the corner. "That spot looks perfect." Gina sat on the leather chair which left only one place for Oscar and Sydney to sit.

The loveseat.

Oscar watched as Sydney's eyes jumped back and forth between Gina and the loveseat.

She pointed to the loveseat. "Sure you don't want to sit over here with me?"

Gina smiled and wiggled her butt in the chair. "I'm comfy here." She winked at Sydney. "Would you two please sit? It's a loveseat, not a bed."

Oscar liked Gina. She was fun and outgoing. He wouldn't be surprised if something happened between her and Leo since they had a lot in common. As for Sydney, he was still waiting for her to sit.

She sat directly in the middle of the loveseat, leaving no room for Oscar on either side of her. She pointed across the way. "Do you want to grab that chair over there and bring it over for yourself?"

Oscar chuckled. "Not particularly." He squeezed into the space on her side and pushed her over with his hip until he had enough room. "There we go. Isn't that nice?"

"Just lovely. You don't give up, do you?"

"Not when I see something I like."

Gina laughed and took a sip of her martini. "How is it you don't have a thick Spanish accent? I remember reading in *People* magazine you were born in Málaga but you haven't been here in the US that long."

"My mother and father both speak five languages and knew I'd have more opportunities in life being bilingual. They arranged classes with native-speaking teachers since preschool and I was bilingual at the age of seven. I'm not sure why, but languages have always come easy to me. I'm also fluent in Italian, although I admit I don't use it much."

"I've always wanted to go to Spain but haven't been there yet."

"You'll love it. The beauty, the history, and especially the people in the South where I'm from." Oscar turned to Sydney, who quietly nursed her drink. "And you, Sunshine? Have you been to Spain?"

Sydney sat up straight and huffed. "Don't call me that. And yes, I've been there. In fact, I was in Málaga exactly eleven summers ago for the celebration of La Noche de San Juan. I wrote a story about it on my travel blog."

Gina set her drink down on the table. "I remember that. That was the party on the beach, right?"

Oscar nodded. "It's more than a party. La Noche de San Juan was one of the biggest celebrations of the year in Spain. Hundreds of thousands of people head to the beach at night to celebrate the longest day of the year with live music, food, and spectacular fireworks."

Sydney took a sip of her drink. "There were bonfires on the beaches. One of the rituals is writing a wish on a piece of paper and tossing it into the fire."

"Did you make a wish that night?" asked Oscar.

She smirked. "Yes, but I'm not going to tell you what it was."

"Of course not. I don't expect you to. But it looks like we have another case of serendipity between us."

"How so?"

"I went back to Spain that summer for a wedding. I was on that beach eleven years ago when you were there."

"I don't believe it."

"You don't think a proud Spanish man would take part in a celebration as big as La Noche de San Juan in his own hometown?"

"I believe you," said Gina.

Oscar scooted forward to the edge of the love seat and held out his glass. "Thank you."

Gina clinked his glass. "It makes perfect sense. That's like not believing a New Yorker who said he was in Times Square on New Year's Eve when the ball dropped."

Sydney took another sip of her gin fizz. "Okay, let's say you were there. How is that serendipity? We didn't meet that day."

"True. But it's quite possible we walked right by each other and didn't even know it. We could have been standing in line buying food at the same time or maybe we even wished the same wish. The universe could have been trying to get us together, but then realized it wasn't time yet. You and I had to go through more of life's lessons before we would be ready for each other."

"What types of life's lessons? The ones where we both get engaged?"

"That's serendipity."

"I swear I'm going to choke the serendipity out of you."

"What are the chances two engaged people are on a cruise to Alaska without their fiancés?"

Sydney shrugged.

"Oscar!" yelled Joanne, approaching with her husband Raymond. "Get over here! I need to give you a big kiss. Thank you for your advice."

Oscar smiled, set his drink glass on the small side table, and stood. Then Joanne gave him a kiss on each cheek.

Raymond stepped forward and also kissed Oscar on both cheeks. "I owe you too, amigo. I'm alive again. Our relationship has changed and it's all because of you! Joanne did a striptease that—"

"Raymond!"

"Oh. Yeah, I guess I shouldn't be talking about that in public. Anyway, thanks."

And just like that they were gone. Oscar took a seat and grabbed his gin fizz, wondering when the demand for more details would come from the feisty woman to his right. It would only be a matter of time.

Oscar actually loved that about women. Men typically complained about how complex women were and how impossible they were to figure out, but he knew them well. He knew what they wanted, even when they said they didn't want it. Most women wanted details. He'd learned that a long time ago. You can't just tell a woman you ran into her friend Rebecca while you were at the store and leave it at that. You'd better have more information because that just wouldn't be good enough. And it wouldn't make sense to her that you didn't *get* more information from her friend. Soon the questions would come flying back at you. And if you didn't have the answers, you would appear to be a fool in her eyes.

"You saw Rebecca?"

"Who was she with?"

"Is little Billy still sick?"

"How come she wasn't working?"

"Did you ask her if she got the message I left her yesterday?"

"Has her dad found a job yet?"

"What was she buying?"

"Did you ask them if they're coming over this weekend for the party?"

"Did you tell her I got the promotion?"

Oscar played it off with Sydney, like what just happened with Joanne and Raymond was no big deal. "This drink is wonderful. Have I told you that?"

Sydney smacked him on the side of the leg. "Oh no, you don't. Explain."

He grinned and played innocent. "Explain what? My love for this drink? No problem. I—"

"Nice try, señor. You know what I mean."

"Oh, you want me to explain Joanne and Raymond?"

"That woman is old enough to be my grandmother. I'd like to know what advice you gave them and why she did a striptease for Grandpa."

"I'd imagine that she did a striptease for him because it

added spontaneity and pleasure to their relationship. Pleasure is good, no?"

The red color appearing on Sydney's face was a good sign. Oscar held out his hand.

Sydney stared at it. "What?"

"Give me your hand. I would like to show you something."

"Nice try."

"Seriously. It's more on the scientific side, but I promise you will be amazed at how something so simple can be so powerful and enjoyable."

Sydney took another sip of her drink. "Show Gina."

Gina popped up out of her seat. "Yes! Show me!"

Sydney was a fool. Why hadn't she given Oscar her hand? She had changed seats with Gina and watched her best friend enjoy whatever Oscar was doing to her. Was it a hand massage? Something with pressure points? She couldn't figure it out.

Gina closed her eyes. "Oh. This is so amazing, Oscar." Gina looked like she was on the verge of having the big O. Disgusting. And that could have been her over there.

Oscar kept his eyes on Sydney as he worked Gina's palm. "The hand has twenty-seven bones if you include the wrist, and three nerves. I'm targeting the sensory nerves and applying pressure at a ninety-degree angle for maximum pleasure."

Maximum pleasure sounded nice.

She tried to remember the last time she had been intimate with Elliot. He was always away on a business trip. She couldn't even remember. It had been weeks, for sure. She missed the human touch. The kisses.

And now she watched as her best friend got special treatment from the sexy Spanish man with the amazing hands.

"I'm in heaven," said Gina.

Enough was enough. Sydney had to have some of that right now.

Sydney popped up from her seat. "Okay, my turn!"

Oscar gave her a *tsk tsk*. "You had your chance."

She frowned. "It's too late?"

"I can check my calendar for tomorrow and see if I have an opening, but my services are in demand, you know?"

"Cruel. That's what you are."

He grinned. "I hope I can make it up to you one day."

Gina opened her eyes and slid her hand out of Oscar's grip. "Okay, you big baby. Go ahead."

"No. I don't want to now."

"Looks like someone needs another drink. Either that or it's past her bedtime."

"Both. But I do want to go to bed early tonight. Tomorrow's one of the highlights of the entire trip and I want to get on deck early for the best spot."

Sydney looked forward to seeing Glacier Bay, a breathtaking national park and preserve with some of the world's most spectacular tidewater glaciers. Cruise ships typically spent a full day cruising the pristine waters of the park including a stop at a major tidewater glacier. Over a half a million visitors come each year to witness the snow-capped mountains, spectacular glaciers, and emerald–green forests. All from the comfort of their cruise ship.

"It's something you'll never forget," said Oscar. "Do you have binoculars?"

Sydney grimaced.

Oscar waved her off. "Don't worry about it. There's an extra pair in my suite. I'll make sure to bring them. Make sure you go to the top—to the Sky View Deck—if you want the best view. But go early because it will get crowded."

"Is that where you'll be?"

He nodded.

Gina clasped her hands together and smiled. "This is so exciting. We'll come find you."

Oscar grinned. "Great. It's a date."

CHAPTER SEVEN

Oscar had gotten up at seven and had breakfast brought to his suite. He'd showered and was ready to head up to the Sky View Deck. Glacier Bay from his balcony was a spectacular sight, but it didn't compare to the view of Sydney St. James. He had thought of asking her to join him in his suite today to view the glaciers, but he was sure she would have thought he wanted to get her into his bed. It wasn't a bad idea, but it honestly hadn't crossed his mind. When he'd first met her he thought it could have been infatuation, but he realized quickly it could become more than that.

He grabbed both binoculars from the top of the bar and took the elevator up to the Sky View Deck. Ships weren't allowed to dock in Glacier Bay, but they did spend most of the day there, moving from one glacier to another. It was one of the highlights of the trip so he shouldn't have been so surprised when the elevator doors opened.

People. Too many people. Everywhere. Don't they eat breakfast?

Hundreds of people were already lined up against the rail, viewing the amazing landscape and snapping photo after photo. Then he figured out the problem. Television crews and professional photographers had blocked off over half of the deck with their equipment.

He made his way through the throngs of people to the front of the ship, searching for Sydney and Gina. It was hard to distinguish one person from another considering everyone was bundled up for protection against the cold. Parkas, gloves, beanies—it looked like many of them were ready for a downhill run on the ski slope. Not a surprise. Although Glacier Bay had many beautiful days, that day they had encountered fog and temperatures at least thirty degrees colder than their last stop, Ketchikan.

He made his way to the port side of the ship and heard a woman yell his name. He turned around but couldn't see where the voice came from. Then he heard it again.

"Oscar! Over here!"

He turned another ninety degrees and spotted a hand waving to him above the heads of the passengers. Gina. And Sydney was smiling next to her.

He made his way to them, cutting in between people and excusing himself a couple of times.

Finally he stood in front of Sydney. "You made it. Why did you invite all these people?"

Sydney laughed. "It's crazy. I think everyone had the same idea you had."

Gina slid over and squeezed in between the two of them. "There's got to be a better way to see this."

"Look at that whale!" someone screamed, prompting people to run toward the voice.

Oscar pointed to the opening against the rail. "Quick! Get in that spot!"

Sydney and Gina jumped and filled in the opening, now occupying a front row spot. Oscar slid in behind them and looked out toward the bay.

He was directly behind Sydney and found it difficult to concentrate on Glacier Bay.

A man looking through binoculars pointed to the mountain across the way and screamed, "A bald eagle!"

A group of people quickly shifted from one side to the other, bumping Oscar into the back of Sydney. He grabbed her shoulders for stability to keep from smashing her. She smelled fantastic, which was surprising, considering she was covered in multiple layers of clothing.

She flipped around and looked into his eyes. "Oh . . ."

Those hazel eyes.

His heart rate accelerated and he removed his arms from her shoulders and smoothed out some of the creases in her jacket. "Sorry. It can get a little crazy here. You okay?"

"Fine. Maybe it's not so crazy on one of the other decks." Sydney looked around and spotted Leo. "Hey, there's the cruise director, Leo. Let's go see if he has a suggestion."

Leo smiled as they approached. "Enjoying the scenery?"

Gina frowned. "To be honest, it's a little crazy at the moment."

Leo nodded. "The press took up more space than we anticipated. Plus, people want to be the first ones to see Glacier Bay. It will thin out as the day goes on, so don't worry. You'll have plenty of time to enjoy the view and take pictures." A helicopter flew overhead and they all looked up. Leo pointed across the bay. "The people on that helicopter are on their way to land on top of one of the glaciers. They're passengers from another cruise."

Sydney watched the helicopter disappear into the fog. "Seriously?"

He nodded. "Oh, yeah. We offer the same excursion that goes out tomorrow morning when we arrive in Juneau."

"Sounds dangerous."

"Not at all—they know what they're doing and they won't go out if the weather is rough. You do need to be careful where you're walking out there, but you have a professional guide with you at all times. There are people who rave about it, but it's not for everyone."

Gina grimaced. "Not for me."

"Me, neither," said Oscar. "Any idea when the fog will clear up?"

Leo took a look across the bay. "Within the hour, most likely." He slapped Oscar on the back. "Okay, gotta run.

The National Park Service rangers just came aboard and are getting ready to do a presentation about the park."

Leo took off and Sydney looked back out toward the bay. She was taller than most women, but still, it wasn't easy to see the glaciers. "Well, what should we do until some of these people get tired or hungry?"

"I have an idea," said Oscar. The thought of inviting Sydney back to his suite popped into his head and his heart rate picked up. It didn't make sense. He'd never had a problem asking a woman out. But this was different. *She* was different. And how could he compare Sydney to other women anyway? Impossible.

"Oscar?"

"Yeah?"

Sydney stared at him with a concerned look on her face. "You said you had an idea. Were you planning on sharing it with us anytime in the near future?"

"Of course . . . I was going to suggest that we go back to my suite and enjoy this magical place from my balcony."

"Oh . . ."

"And in case you're wondering, I only have the best intentions. I'm inviting you so you can truly enjoy Glacier Bay without the possibility of being crushed to death by the passengers around you."

Sydney laughed. "Thanks for clarifying that but I don't want to leave Gina here by herself. I'm here because of her and it wouldn't seem right."

Gina turned around. "I'm a big girl—go have fun. I'll be okay."

Oscar held up his hand. "No, no. I should have been more clear. My invitation was for Gina as well. Of course."

He liked the surprised look on Sydney's face. That was good to see. Maybe she would open up and trust him more.

Sydney nodded. "Gina? What do you think?"

"I'm in. There's enough room on your balcony for the three of us?"

And a hundred other people. "Yes. Shouldn't be a problem."

Gina smiled and gestured toward the door to go inside. "What are we waiting for?"

Gina mouthed *so sexy* to Sydney as they followed Oscar to his suite. Sydney gave her a look and mouthed *stop it* to her best friend. They got in the elevator and went down a couple of floors.

After they left the elevator, they continued to walk toward the end of the long hallway and Sydney noticed how far the doors were spaced apart. "These suites must be huge."

They arrived at Oscar's suite and Gina pointed to the wall next to the door. "The man has a doorbell! Who has a doorbell on a cruise ship?" Gina laughed. "That's funny." She pulled out her smartphone and took a picture.

Oscar chuckled, opened the door, and waved them through. "After you."

Sydney followed Gina inside and they both froze in the entryway.

Gina placed her hand on her chest. "You've got to be kidding me . . ."

Sydney was about to say the same thing. Their eyes traveled around the suite, which seemed like a town home. There was a bar, a library, a fireplace, and an entertainment center with what must have been a hundred-inch television. The dining room table had chairs for eight people.

Gina screamed. "You have a baby grand piano! This place is ridiculous. And what's that?" She pointed up. "No way . . ."

Sydney laughed and eyed the loft. The man had a loft in his cabin. Sorry . . . his *suite*.

Gina followed Sydney's eyes up to the loft. "A king-sized bed!"

Oscar shrugged. "It's a bit much?"

"Not at all," said Sydney. "I'm feeling a little claustrophobic, actually."

Oscar laughed, then winked and gestured to the balcony. "Let's go enjoy the view from the balcony."

Sydney and Gina followed Oscar. On the way she noticed his fancy camera on the counter. A professional camera for sure, which surprised her. Why didn't he have it with him when he was on the Sky View Deck?

She pointed to the camera. "Don't you want to bring your camera?"

He glanced over at the counter and crinkled his nose.

"Not right now. Let's go outside." He turned back around and headed out to the balcony.

The way he answered didn't sit right with her. There was something he wasn't saying.

Gina screamed again. "Sydney! Get out here!"

Sydney laughed and stepped through the sliding glass door.

Gina pointed to the Jacuzzi. "Look!"

Sydney glanced around at the enormous balcony. Oscar's suite was outrageous, but his balcony was insane. She tapped him on the arm. "When Gina asked you about us all fitting on your balcony, you said it shouldn't be a problem. That was a slight understatement, considering we could fit the Mormon Tabernacle Choir here."

Oscar laughed. "I didn't want it to seem as if I was bragging."

Gina's eyes traveled around from the outdoor dining table to the lounge chairs to the Jacuzzi. "I'm so blown away by this."

Oscar nodded. "I hope you haven't forgotten the reason we're here." He pointed to the giant glacier almost directly in front of them. The three of them moved toward the rail and were silent for a few moments, admiring the scenery and the crystal clear water. "This particular glacier is called Margerie and is over sixteen miles long. And if we wait long enough we can usually see—"

A colossal chunk of ice dropped from Margerie Glacier into the sea, creating a cannon-like boom.

Sydney jumped back in awe of the power. "That was

amazing. Gina, did you get a picture of that?"

"Yeah, but you should take pictures, too, just in case."

Sydney turned to Oscar. "Can you get your camera?"

He shook his head. "Not right now."

She studied him for a moment. "Why not?"

He shrugged. "To be honest, it's been over ten years since I turned that camera on."

"And you forgot where the power button was?"

He chuckled. "No."

"So mysterious . . . But you enjoyed taking pictures back then?"

"It was all I thought about. Taking pictures was my passion."

"I don't get it. How can you love something so much and then give up on it, just like that?"

Oscar didn't answer.

Sydney pointed to the inside of the suite. "Get the camera."

"That's quite all right."

"Do me a favor."

"Anything for you . . . except the camera."

She smacked him on his arm. "I want a nice photo with the glacier behind me. Our smartphone cameras just won't do. Are you going to deny me that?"

"You want me to take a picture of you with my camera?" She nodded. "And then what will I do with the picture?"

She smiled. "That's up to you. You can keep it for yourself, but ideally I'd like a copy."

He nodded and went inside the suite without saying another word. A minute later he returned with the camera in hand.

Sydney moved toward the rail and made sure the glacier was behind her. "How's this?"

He turned the camera on, made a few adjustments and then looked through the viewfinder. "You don't need to do anything at all. Just smile and I'll adjust the shot from my end."

"Sounds great." She smiled and waited but he didn't take a photograph. He looked a little disturbed and she could see him take in a deep breath. What was going on with him? "Are you okay?"

"I'm fine. Sorry. Try again. Smile."

She smiled and he snapped a shot. She turned sideways and smiled again. "How's this?"

"Perfect."

She felt like a supermodel, striking different poses for the photographer.

"Hey!" said Gina, scooting in next to Sydney. "You can't have all the fun!"

Oscar snapped a few pictures of the two of them and then turned the camera toward one of the mountains. "Just one moment . . ."

Sydney moved next to Oscar. "What is it?"

Oscar pulled the viewfinder away from his eye and clicked a button on the back of the camera to display the photo he had just taken. Then he turned the back of the camera to Sydney.

Sydney's mouth fell open as she moved closer. "Is that? No way..."

Gina moved closer. "What is it?" She leaned closer and eyed the camera screen. "A bear!"

Sydney looked back over toward the meadow across the water but couldn't see it. Then she used the binoculars and found it. "I see it!" She took her attention away from the bear and glanced at Oscar. "How did you know it was there? I couldn't even see it without the binoculars."

"You have to know what to look for. The trick is to look for some type of movement or unusual shapes, then use the binoculars or the zoom of the camera to get a closer look. Bears often forage on the beach or in the meadows near the shore."

"Amazing."

Sydney raised the binoculars again and scanned Glacier Bay. The ship began to turn in a different direction, showing a completely different glacier.

Oscar pointed to it. "That is Lamplugh Glacier. It also travels sixteen miles to reach the sea. If you look closely you can see a cave right in the middle of the face."

Sydney zoomed in with the binoculars. "Oh yeah, I see it." She pulled the binoculars away from her eyes. "Are you sure you don't have roots in Alaska? You know so much about this place."

"Remember I've been here before. Plus, I've always been curious and fascinated about the world, the beautiful places and cultures. I could travel all year round."

"Me, too."

He had a spark in his eye and his glance dropped to her lips. She eyed his luscious Spanish mouth and then turned back toward the bay, raising the binoculars back up to her eyes. She didn't want to give him the wrong impression, but had to wonder what his kisses were like. Probably like heaven considering how passionate he was. But what was she doing? She needed to quit thinking about his kisses.

Bad girl!

Two hours later, they were still on the balcony. They'd seen most of the major glaciers in the bay and a handful of breaching whales. They chatted about places they'd like to visit in the world. Oscar asked her about her dreams and goals. Elliot had never asked her that. He just wanted to talk about his job.

Sydney and Oscar had so much in common.

She stared out at the emerald waters and took in a deep breath of the crisp, fresh air. She hadn't felt this relaxed in a long time.

Gina jumped up and turned to Sydney and Oscar. "I'm heading downstairs to wander around. Thank you, Oscar. This was amazing."

"My pleasure."

Sydney enjoyed the balcony way too much to leave but she wouldn't mention it to Gina or give her a hard time. She stood and—

"You don't have to leave, too," Gina added. "Sit back down. Relax."

She didn't have a problem with that.

She slid back into the lounge chair and sighed. "Okay."

After Gina left, Sydney turned to Oscar. "I wanted to say thank you as well. This is wonderful."

"You're welcome."

They both turned their attention back to the bay. A few seconds, later a humpback whale breached in front of them. This time its entire body was airborne.

Sydney jumped up and ran to the edge of the balcony, with Oscar right behind her. That had to be one of the most beautiful things she'd ever seen.

The whale breached again and she sighed. "This place is magical. I can't believe I'm here." She laughed. "Actually I can't believe I'm here with you."

"Serendipity."

Sydney huffed. "Here we go again. I'm sure that works well on other women but I don't believe in serendipity."

"How else do you explain our chance encounters? The Sweet Tooth Cafe where you almost killed me with an eclair?" Sydney laughed. "The captain's dinner? The pool? Surely you don't think these are all coincidences."

"I do, except for the captain's dinner since the cruise director is your best friend. You obviously arranged that."

He nodded. "I did. What about the swimming pool?"

"Coincidence."

He thought about it for a minute. "I'd like to try an experiment."

"With my hand? You had your chance."

"So did you, but I was thinking of something a little more adventurous. First, do you have an excursion planned for tomorrow in Juneau?"

"No. Gina and I had planned on trying to book one before we left home but we were just too busy. We were going to look at the options tonight and maybe book something."

"Perfect. I don't have anything planned yet either."

Sydney turned her head to the side. "Okay, you've lost me."

He held his hand out. "Please come with me. I'll show you."

Sydney took his hand and Oscar led her inside. "Okay . . ."

She'd be lying if she said she didn't enjoy the way he held onto her hand. She loved his confidence and his take-charge personality. Communication wasn't one of his flaws and she'd never have to wonder what was on his mind. She liked that.

Oscar grabbed the brochure from the top of the baby grand piano and held it up for her to see. "These are the excursions for tomorrow. Now here's what I suggest. You pick something and book it. Don't tell me what it is. Then . . . I'll pick something and book it without telling *you* what it is. Would you believe in serendipity if we both ended up on the same excursion?"

She stared at the brochure for a few moments and shrugged. "What are the choices?"

"Great question. Let's see . . ." He opened the brochure and browsed through the activities. "Okay, we have some good ones here. Snorkeling—"

She jerked her head back. "Snorkeling in Alaska?

That's crazy. No way."

Oscar laughed. "Please don't tell me your opinion of any of these. I want this to be fair. Otherwise you'll make up some excuse when our serendipity becomes a reality and I want you to be completely convinced."

His confidence gave her an odd sensation in her stomach. Nerves. What if he was right? What if they ended up picking the same excursion? She shook the possibility out of her head. No way that would happen.

Oscar flicked the side of the brochure with his finger. "Pay attention here, this is important."

"*Very* important," she said, making sure her comment oozed with as much sarcasm as she could add to it.

"Good. Your choices are snorkeling, dog sledding, whale watching, nature tour, helicopter glacier landing, city tour, and salmon fishing."

She smiled. "I think I already know which one I want to do."

"Great. Go ahead and book it sometime today and I'll do the same."

"There's no way we would pick the same one."

"How do you know?"

"I know."

Oscar nodded. "Okay, if you're so confident I'd like to propose something. If we pick the same excursion, I want you to have lunch with me in Victoria when we stop there in two days. And I can introduce you to someone special there."

"Another fiancée?"

Oscar chuckled. "Not quite."

"By the way, where *is* your fiancée? It's odd she's not with you."

He shrugged. "Maybe not so odd. Your fiancé is not here, either."

"This is my bachelorette party. Gina is my maid of honor and this trip was a gift from her."

"You're lucky to have such a wonderful friend like her."

"I agree."

She waited for him to respond with the reason why his fiancée wasn't on the ship, but it never came.

Oscar smiled. "Let's get back to my proposal. If we pick the same excursion, you'll let me take you to lunch in Victoria."

"I don't know . . ."

"If you're so certain that this is not serendipity, you have nothing to lose."

"And how do I know you won't ask Leo what I've picked? He must have access to all the passengers' information."

"He does—definitely. But I give you my word that I won't cheat." He held out his hand.

Sydney glanced down at it and hesitated. Then she grabbed it and shook. She loved his smile, his touch. But enough was enough.

She looked down and sighed. "Can I have my hand back?"

He chuckled. "Of course. For now."

CHAPTER EIGHT

"I'm not getting in a helicopter!" Gina said, her hands on her hips. "You're on your own if you choose that excursion."

Gina wanted to go on the nature tour excursion instead. Heck, if it wasn't for Oscar's obsession with serendipity Sydney would have chosen the nature tour as well. But the Spaniard had looked so confident when he'd talked about serendipity she wanted to prove him wrong.

She and Gina had carefully analyzed all the excursions, trying to figure out which one Oscar wouldn't pick. They remembered the conversation when the helicopter had flown over them while they were on the Sky View Deck in Glacier Bay. Oscar had said that type of excursion wasn't for him. His face practically had turned white, which was a surprise because she'd come to the conclusion that that man was the most confident person she'd ever met. He wasn't scared of anything. That's why she was sure he wouldn't pick the helicopter glacier landing excursion.

Sydney paced back and forth in their cabin. "He won't pick the excursion he wants to go on. He'll pick the one he thinks *I* will go on. That's not serendipity. That's psychology. And that's why I can't go on the nature tour. I need to pick the one he doesn't think I would go on *or* the one he would never go on."

"Are you trying to confuse me on purpose? And why are you trying so hard to try to prove him wrong? Why not choose what you really want to do and see what happens? It would be fascinating to see if his theory was real. Imagine you and Oscar as a couple."

She *had* imagined that. The dream last night seemed so real.

Too real.

She and Oscar were married, traveling the world together, having the time of their lives. And no matter the hour, the day, or where they were, he was always kissing her. Cherishing her. The surprising part was after she'd gotten up in the middle of the night to pee. When she'd gotten back in bed and had fallen asleep, the dream had continued exactly where it had left off. They lived in a house by the ocean and had children. Two beautiful Spanish-American girls with big brown eyes they had gotten from their daddy. She'd never had a dream about Elliot like that. Maybe she lived in a fantasy world like the millions of other women around the world who had a crush on Oscar. But why did she think it was more than that?

Gina pointed to Sydney's face. "You're thinking about him, aren't you?"

"No! Okay, yes! And part of me wants to pick what I really want to do but that part of me is also scared. Because I have a feeling he'll be there and then what do I do?"

"Follow your heart."

"This is my bachelorette party and we haven't talked about Elliot since we boarded the ship."

"Maybe that's a sign. If I was getting married you wouldn't be able to shut me up about my fiancé."

"Thanks a lot!"

"Hey, I wanted to go to Vegas for a couple days and party. You're the one who forced me to come on this cruise. But now that I'm here I'm enjoying myself, I want you to know that." She smiled and squeezed Sydney's shoulder. "And you know I only want the best for you. Just don't fight it. If you want to explore this thing with Oscar, you should do that. Find out if it's cold feet or something real, because you need to be sure about marriage with Elliot, too. The last thing you want is to get a divorce six months later and then find out you lost your chance of being with Oscar because your best friend just had his baby."

Sydney grabbed the pillow from the bed and flung it at Gina. "You're so bad."

"Hey, if you won't go for him, I will."

"I'll kill you if you end up on the excursion with Oscar while I'm stuck on a glacier all by myself. And if you have his baby I'll kill you twice!"

"Why do you care? You're the one trying to avoid him!

AN ECLAIR TO REMEMBER

Anyway, you've got nothing to worry about. As handsome as Oscar is, I'm more attracted to Leo. But that's the beauty of life! There's someone for everyone. You didn't plan this but you shouldn't fight it. And if you truly think that coming on this cruise was a big mistake—not because you're scared but because you know the best thing in the world is waiting for you at home at this moment—then let's head to the Juneau airport right now and catch the next flight back."

Right. Sydney had no interest in returning home.

Thirty minutes later, she disembarked from the ship and waited at the port with four other people in front of the shuttle van with the sign marked *Helicopter Glacier Landing*. She'd never been on a helicopter in her entire life but felt proud she would overcome her fear and just do it. She smiled thinking of the conversation she'd had with Gina this morning.

She looked for her best friend in the other lines but the port was a madhouse with literally hundreds and hundreds of people lined up in front of the countless excursion shuttles. She looked for Oscar as well, but he was nowhere in sight.

She adjusted the scarf around her neck and waited. They had informed her she needed to dress warmly in layers and not to forget sunglasses, gloves, and the camera. Check, check, and check.

She was ready to go.

The driver opened the door to the van and checked everyone's IDs. He took their excursion vouchers and told them to take a seat inside the van. Sydney and the four other adventurers entered the van and sat on their seats, waiting for their adventure.

The driver peeked inside the open door of the van. "Just waiting on one more person and we'll be on our way."

Sydney stared at the empty seat next to her. There was no way they were waiting for Oscar. It was impossible he would be on that excursion.

"Sorry I'm late," said the Spanish man, practically diving through the open door of the van.

She shook her head. How did he do that? Gina said he'd made it clear he would never do this type of excursion. Did he set her up? But how? Did Gina tell him? He was a genius, so maybe she shouldn't be surprised this happened.

"Oscar Martin?" asked the driver.

Oscar handed the driver his ID and voucher. "Yes."

A few seconds later, he walked to the back of the van and sat in the open seat next to Sydney.

"Here we go!" said the driver. He closed the van door and drove onto the main road toward the airport.

Oscar turned to Sydney and grinned. "Beautiful day to walk on a glacier, wouldn't you say?"

"Just peachy."

She tried to play it off, but deep down inside she was glad to see him. What was it about this Spaniard that made her heart race? She was normally the most confident woman in the room, but around him she was a complete mess. She had even cried twice and she *never* did that. Who was she kidding? This guy had all the qualities of a man she'd be interested in. Except for that part where he was engaged.

She turned and eyed his dark green down parka with the fur-trimmed hood, then dropped her gaze down to his black jeans and hiking boots. The man knew how to dress himself, which was a good thing.

He turned and gave her a grin she would never get tired of. "Are you looking for something in particular?"

Heat crawled up Sydney's neck to her face. "No. Just checking out your clothes. You look . . . comfortable."

"I am."

"Tell me how you figured out I would choose this excursion. You talked with Leo, didn't you?"

"I gave you my word I wouldn't talk to him."

"Then it was Gina, right?"

"No. Not her either."

"I don't believe you."

"Honesty is something you will always get from me. It's the highest form of intimacy."

Great. Oscar Martin was talking about intimacy. She pictured that king-sized bed in the loft of his suite. That seemed like a lovely place to get intimate. And she needed to get his bed out of her thoughts!

It was his fault her mind went there. He needed to learn how to control his vocabulary. Using words like intimacy was cruel and unusual punishment. Or more like torture since she hadn't had sex in such a long time.

Oscar glanced out the window and watched as their shuttle van passed a sign for Juneau International Airport.

"Okay, I'll tell you why I picked this excursion but then you will argue it's not serendipity. I didn't choose it because it was the one I wanted to go on the most. I chose it because I knew you would choose it. I originally wanted to go on a different tour."

"We saw the look on your face when Leo talked about landing a helicopter. You didn't have a happy face. So what, you'd suffer just to prove me wrong?"

"No. I'd suffer just to spend more time with you."

Damn him and his romantic ways. No wonder women all over the world went gaga for Oscar.

"Which excursion did you originally want to go on?" she couldn't help but ask. She wanted to know but she didn't want to know. Because if he said nature tour she was going to scream.

"The nature tour."

"No way!"

The driver slammed on the brakes. The woman in the back screamed as a couple of cars behind them honked their horns. Oscar stuck his arm out in front of Sydney's chest to prevent her from flying forward and ended up copping a feel in the process. She tried to get a good read on him. He was trying to hold in laughter.

The driver looked in the rearview mirror. "Is everything okay?"

"Yes. Sorry about that." Sydney glanced over at Oscar again. "Don't you dare laugh."

"Me? Never. I'm a serious person." His bottom lip quivered. "Serendipity."

She gestured to his sexy mouth. "Don't do that. Let's change subjects." She pointed to his small bag. "You brought your camera?"

He nodded. "Yes. Thanks to you."

She stared at him for a moment. "What did I do?"

"For some reason you motivated me when you asked me how someone could give up on something they were passionate about. I thought about it and you were right. I don't know what happened, really. Okay, I take that back—maybe I do. I got caught up in a new life and new responsibilities. The photography went on the back burner."

"Living that Hollywood lifestyle must be time consuming."

He glanced around at the other passengers in the van and leaned in to Sydney. "You don't really believe everything you read, do you? Or what you see on the television gossip shows?"

"When everyone starts talking about it, it's not easy to dismiss as false."

"Okay," said the driver. "Everyone head inside."

Sydney glanced through the windshield of the van. The company's headquarters was located inside an old barn at the airport. Hopefully, the helicopters were more modern than their office. After the pre-flight safety video, all the passengers were weighed. They used that information to assign seats and evenly distribute the weight in the helicopter. They slipped on glacier boots over their shoes, placed their personal things in the lockers, and fifteen minutes later were in the air. She enjoyed the music pumping through the headphones she'd received. Occasionally the pilot would interrupt the music to talk about the landing or the landscape below.

Soaring over the Juneau Icefield was spectacular from their seats. They had great views out of the side windows of the aircraft. The panoramic view of the frozen wonderland was amazing. Sydney took photos of the lush forests, glassy alpine lakes, jagged mountain peaks and rock formations. She'd never seen anything like it in the world.

She glanced over at Oscar. The man was doing something he was dead-set against just to be with her. She wondered if he regretted coming. He had a dull look in his eyes as he stared off into the distance. He gripped the armrest so hard it looked like he was going to snap it off.

Something was definitely wrong.

CHAPTER NINE

Maybe this wasn't such a smart idea. Oscar took pride in being able to overcome just about any obstacle that came his way in life. Fear wasn't part of his vocabulary. He thought by choosing this excursion he would be able to spend some quality time with Sydney and get to know her better. He also thought he would be able to block out the past. He didn't expect his mind to obsess over his best friend's death ten years ago. He thought he had moved on and accepted his death, but once the helicopter had taken off the past had returned and invaded his head like a swarm of bees—attacking from every direction.

He needed to snap out of it. He didn't like the way Sydney looked at him, like he was pathetic.

Luckily, the pilot gently set the helicopter down on one of the ancient rivers of ice. They followed his guidance and stepped out of the aircraft and onto Taku Glacier, a tidewater glacier southeast of Juneau. The fog had cleared and it was an absolutely beautiful day. He took a deep breath and felt better. That little episode had passed and now he could enjoy the beauty around him.

Sydney approached Oscar and rubbed the side of his arm. "Are you okay? You didn't look so hot up there."

He nodded. "I'm just peachy, as you say. Much better now."

"Do you have a fear of flying?"

"No." She watched him, obviously waiting for more but he wouldn't give it to her. This wasn't the time to talk about that. She was on top of a glacier and needed to enjoy the experience. He gestured around the glacier. "What do you think?"

Sydney smiled and did a three-sixty. "We've landed on the moon."

"And *you* are the most beautiful astronaut I've ever met."

She pointed her finger at Oscar. "Don't you start."

The pilot waved them all over to a channel of clear water flowing under his feet. He pulled out a handful of straws and passed one to each person. "Thirsty? You won't get many opportunities in life to drink pure glacier water straight from the source. Here's what you need to do . . ." He lay down flat on the ice on his stomach and leaned part of his head into the channel with the straw in his mouth. Then he sucked in some water through the straw. "Ahhh, the best, most refreshing water in the world. Okay, your turn. Enjoy! We have only twenty minutes here, so make the most of it. Explore, take lots of pictures, and watch your step."

Oscar lay down flat on his stomach and copied the pilot's technique, taking a sip of fresh glacier water through the straw. The pilot was right—it was the best. He popped back up on his feet, pleased to know Sydney had been watching him.

He gestured to the water. "Your turn."

Sydney smiled, got on her stomach and bent her neck so her head hung down over the water. Then she took a sip using the straw and licked her lips. "Amazing."

He agreed. Her lips were amazing.

Oscar held his hand out for her and helped her back to her feet. "Magnificent."

She glanced around the glacier and surrounding hills. "I agree."

"I meant you."

They held each other's gazes for a moment. The silence had so much energy.

Oscar glanced down at her lips and then grinned. "I look forward to our lunch tomorrow in Victoria."

She smirked. "I never agreed to that lunch."

"You never said no, either."

"True."

"You're attracted to me . . ."

"Is that a question?"

"No. The problem is I may be more attracted to you than you are to me."

Sydney laughed and pulled her gloved hand from his.

"Right . . . I doubt that." She threw her hand over her mouth. "You didn't hear me say that."

"I didn't?"

"No. In fact, I'll make myself disappear."

"You're a magician now? This I would love to see."

She wandered off toward the open area below the hill, the only one out there. She glanced back at him and stuck her tongue out.

Playful. He loved that.

He loved watching her. She moved carefully across the ice and then stopped, staring up into the hills. Who could blame her for really taking the time to admire such beauty? It had been ten years since he'd been to Alaska and he had missed it. Being surrounded by nature made him feel alive. Combine that with shooting pictures and he was in heaven. He didn't think life could get any better until he'd met Sydney.

Oscar pressed the power button on the camera. The back display illuminated and he adjusted a few of the settings. He glanced back up at Sydney who was still fixated on something up on the rocky part of the hill. He snapped a couple of shots of Sydney standing still and inspected them. They looked good. Color balance was right on and the focus on the side of her face was perfect.

There was movement above her on the hill, a small white ball. In his experience, usually that ball was the head of a bald eagle. He used his camera viewfinder to zoom in and see if his instincts were correct. They were. Not a surprise since there were over thirty thousand bald eagles in the state. But what he really hoped was for the bird to take flight. There was nothing like watching an eagle soar across the sky.

He waited patiently. "Come on . . . Time to fly."

A moment later, his wish came true.

The bald eagle jumped off the rocky edge and flapped its large wings, heading right in the direction of Sydney. Then the flapping stopped and the eagle glided effortlessly with the help of the light breeze and its humongous wingspan, almost seven feet wide.

Sydney had her neck arched and looked up into the sky, admiring the eagle. Funny. She looked like the eagle with the white beanie on her head and her furry brown winter jacket. As the bird flew directly over Sydney's head, she stretched her arms out to her side to mimic the bird's wingspan. Oscar rapid-fired forty shots. The eagle circled around and flew right back over her head, this time lower. He snapped off another round of shots and continued to shoot as the eagle flew away. He pulled the camera from his face and smiled. He felt so alive shooting those photos. He wanted to shoot more. He smiled, thinking about what just happened. It was rare that a bald eagle would fly so close to a human being. It was like it was attracted to Sydney.

That bird would have to wait in line.

Sydney turned around and smiled, running in his direction. "Did you see that? It was so amazing!"

He had seen it all right. And he was pretty sure one of those photos he'd just taken was the shot of a lifetime.

He smiled back. "Yes! Incredible . . . Another serendipity! We were supposed to be here to witness that!"

She nodded. "You think so?"

"I know so." He pointed to his camera. "I even got some photos."

"Let me see."

He chuckled. "Later. We only have a few more minutes here, so we need to take advantage of the time."

That wasn't the real reason why Oscar didn't want to show her the photos. He wanted to frame one and give it to her as a gift when they got back home.

Sydney sighed. "This is wonderful. No regrets coming?"

"No regrets. It was the best decision ever."

"Why didn't you take something for your air sickness?"

He wasn't going to say anything but she deserved to know. "It wasn't air sickness. One of my dear friends died here. In this spot."

"Oh . . . I'm so sorry."

He took a deep breath and said a silent goodbye to Alberto. "Thank you."

"What happened?"

"I was a freelance photographer and was contracted to come here and shoot publicity photos for the tourism board. I looked forward to it but my sister ended up in the hospital, so I had cut the trip short and canceled the photo shoot. My best friend at the time, Alberto, took my place—he was also a photographer. A good one. Anyway, Alberto was on the helicopter coming here when it crashed. Just like that he was gone."

"Wow . . ."

"This is my first time returning to Alaska since then. I should have been on the helicopter that day. That should have been me who died."

Sydney shook her head. "Not according to your serendipity philosophy. For some reason, it had to be that way."

He nodded. "So I could meet you?"

She wagged her finger at him and smiled. "I knew it wouldn't be long before we were back to that."

"I *am* here on this glacier because of you. Don't forget."

"I'm sure if I forget you'll remind me."

Oscar laughed. "And I'll also remind you how wonderful you are."

"Thank you."

"Are your red cheeks from the cold or from my compliment?"

She shook her head and pushed him away. "Go shoot some pictures, would you?"

Oscar ended up shooting another hundred pictures over the next ten minutes before the pilot alerted them it was time to go. This was a day that would change the course of his life—he was sure of it. His passion for photography had returned and he owed it all to Sydney. He needed to show her just how grateful he was.

"Have dinner with me this evening."

Sydney stopped short of the helicopter and watched the others get on. She appeared deep in thought. "Why?"

"I want to show my appreciation for what you've done for me today."

"It's not necessary."

"From my point of view it is. After Alberto died, I didn't think I would ever pick up that camera again. Then you came along, and just like that, I picked it up. You're a miracle worker."

"No. I'm a magician, remember?"

Oscar chuckled. "A simple dinner, nothing else. Please don't deny me the pleasure of showing you my gratitude."

"A simple dinner?"

"Nothing more."

Sydney eyed the lobster sitting on the platter in front of her. "This is your idea of simple?"

Oscar smiled and tied the bib around his neck. "I assure you these are not complicated to prepare." He lifted his wine glass. "To serendipity."

Sydney lifted her glass and smiled. "You don't give up."

He winked. "I don't."

She toasted Oscar and took a sip of her wine. She glanced around the intimate restaurant. It must have been the most expensive place on the ship and there were only around fifteen tables. The lights were dim and candles were lit on the tables. Just enough light to illuminate the handsome man across from her. Oscar was dressed like he was on his way to a magazine photo shoot, in his European-cut black suit, white shirt, and red necktie. She was glad she'd put on her elegant red evening dress, but wondered if he would say it was serendipity that they matched.

They enjoyed a wonderful dinner and chatted mostly about Alaska and the fascinating place that it was.

Oscar wiped his mouth and smiled. "Delicious. And I want to thank you for not spilling on me or smashing something into my face."

"The night's still young."

Oscar laughed as a staff member stepped forward to clear the plates.

The waiter returned and handed them dessert menus. "I recommend the chocolate Kahlua lava cake this evening. It's one of my favorites."

Oscar frowned. "You don't have eclairs?"

"I'm sorry we don't. They do offer them as well as other delectable, mouth-watering treats and coffee at The Sweet Tooth Cafe."

Oscar handed the menu back to the waiter. "I almost died in that cafe the first evening. I was attacked by another guest—a beautiful woman, in fact."

The waiter's eyes grew wide. "So sorry, sir."

Sydney smacked Oscar on the arm with the menu and then handed it to the waiter. "He's kidding. I'll have the lava cake and a cup of coffee."

"I'd like the same," said Oscar.

"Good choice."

The waiter walked away and Sydney leaned forward. "That guy is going to have nightmares."

"He had to be warned. You should have seen the woman."

"Can we say *hasta la vista* to that joke? It has run its course."

"I think you're right. And I love your Spanish. I know you mentioned you've been to Málaga but have you been to other parts of Spain?"

"Just Madrid. That's why I'm looking forward to going back for our—" Sydney broke eye contact with Oscar. "Uh..."

Oscar leaned lower to try to connect with her eyes. "Going back for your...?"

She should have known she couldn't have avoided the topic forever. She really didn't want to talk about Elliot or her honeymoon. Or anything that had to do with back home. This was her escape and she had been enjoying it.

But now she had guilt.

Oscar was waiting, so she had to say something. "For our honeymoon."

"Ahhh. Yes. That."

She decided to give him a little more info. "One month in Europe, which includes Italy, France, and Spain. And to answer your question, the plan was to go to Barcelona and the Canary Islands."

"Both great choices."

The waiter returned with two chocolate lava cakes on a platter. A second waiter approached and poured the

Kahlua over the dessert. He flicked the switch on the lighter, sending flames shooting upward.

Oscar and Sydney leaned back in their seats and watched the flames dance on top of the lava cake. After the flames faded the waiter placed their desserts in front of them. "Enjoy."

Not surprisingly, they didn't speak much during dessert.

Oscar finished first and pushed the plate away, resting his elbows on the table. "Up until the honeymoon topic I'd say it was an incredible day."

Sydney forced a smile. "I agree."

"Would you like to join me back in my suite for a cup of tea? It's a full moon tonight and there are blankets and outdoor heaters on the balcony."

It sounded heavenly but she couldn't do it. There was too much temptation and she didn't trust herself alone with the man in his suite. Plus the guilt in her gut killed any hope of a romantic evening.

She really had to analyze what she was getting herself into here. Her life was shifting in another direction. Something strong was developing with Oscar, feelings she'd never had before. One thing was certain, no matter what happened with Oscar, she couldn't see herself marrying Elliot. She'd now had a taste of what it was like to feel wanted and craved more.

"Sydney?"

She frowned. "Sorry. It's been a long day and I'd like to

go to bed early. Plus I want to spend some time with Gina."

He nodded and smiled. "You're a good friend. And tomorrow? We're still on for lunch in Victoria, I hope?"

"Yes."

Hopefully, the guilt would be gone by then.

CHAPTER TEN

The next morning Sydney felt better. The guilt had faded away after another pep talk from Gina last night. She had told Sydney to go enjoy the beautiful city of Victoria and not think so much. Her friend was confident everything would become clear to her soon. The good news was Sydney wouldn't have to feel guilty about Gina being all alone on the cruise. Gina had ended up having lunch with Leo yesterday and they really hit it off. Not a surprise. Sydney knew it wouldn't take long for her to meet someone.

Sydney enjoyed Oscar's company and had seen a vulnerable side to him she'd liked as well. Yes, his confidence was appealing, but she also appreciated a man who showed his true self, his insecurities, his fears. Television news programs had built up this image of Oscar Martin almost as a super hero, a man who could do anything. A man who could push obstacles aside with his pinky finger and conquer the world. When you see things enough you start to believe them.

Sydney disembarked from the ship at eleven and waited for Oscar at their agreed location, alongside the water next to the tourism information booth. She had no idea what he had planned or the mysterious person she would meet, but she looked forward to a full day there.

Oscar approached with a grin on his face. "Good morning." He eyed her white skirt and lavender blouse and then looked down at his own clothes. "This is interesting. What are the chances?"

Sydney held up her hand. "Don't say it."

"Fine, fine. I won't say it." He laughed. "But you know I'll be thinking it, right?"

Sydney smacked him on the arm. "Believe me, I know."

They matched perfectly. The man wore white pants and a lavender shirt.

Oscar pulled his smartphone from his pocket. "Hang on, this needs to be documented."

"Our clothes?"

"Yes! This is not a coincidence." He stretched his arm out in front of him with the phone for a selfie. "Smile and pretend you like me."

"That won't be difficult," she mumbled.

"What?"

"Nothing."

They both smiled and Oscar took the picture. "There! Let me make sure it turned out okay." He tapped the picture on his phone and smiled. "Look at us . . . We look happy and harmonious." He showed the picture to her.

Happy and harmonious. Good choice of words. And he was right—they looked good together. Like they were a couple.

"You approve?" he asked.

She nodded. "I approve."

"Good. Me, too." He gestured down the sidewalk to the right. "This way . . ."

They walked down Dallas Road along the shore of Juan de Fuca Strait.

"Oscar!" called out a male voice.

Oscar and Sydney turned around and watched as a man approached out of breath, his wife sheepishly trailing behind.

Oscar smiled. "Hello."

"I thought that was you. What a pleasure it is to meet you!"

"Thank you. And your name is?"

"Oh! John Billman. I'm a big, big fan. I saw the work you did on that high speed jet. It's brilliant. A one hour flight from Los Angeles to Paris would be out of this world."

"Thank you. In due time . . ."

John pulled the cell phone out of his pocket so fast, like it was on fire. "We need to do a selfie! My friends in the Rotary Club are *not* going to believe this!"

Sydney held out her hand. "I can take the photo."

"Great!"

John handed Sydney the phone and wrapped his arm around Oscar, pulling him in tight. "Say cheese."

"Cheese," said Oscar, not at all looking annoyed by the stranger. He'd obviously done this before many times.

They said their goodbyes and Sydney and Oscar continued down Dallas Road.

"That doesn't bug you? Complete strangers wanting to talk to you and take pictures with you?"

"It's expected when you're in the public eye. I'm used to it, I guess. Now if I were having a more intimate moment with a special feisty woman I met on the cruise that would be different."

"Feisty?"

Oscar laughed and pointed to the crosswalk. They crossed the street and walked along the edge of Beacon Hill Park, past the ponds filled with swans, ducks, and blue herons.

"Almost there. Just a little bit more." Oscar gestured to the neighborhood. "This is known as the Heritage Home District. Many of these houses were built in the late 1800s and early 1900s."

Sydney admired the houses as they continued to walk. "They're beautiful. And the mysterious person we're going to visit lives in one of these?"

"Yes."

"And are you going to tell me who this person is?"

He nodded. "Right now." He stopped on the sidewalk and turned toward the brick-colored Victorian home. It was a two-story with white Corinthian columns. "Isabella!"

A woman with wavy chestnut hair and deep brown eyes that matched Oscar's popped out from behind the row of rose trees and delphiniums that lined the front yard. "Hermanito!" She smiled and then yelled back toward the house. "Ben! Oscar is here!" She reached over and grabbed a cane and walked toward Oscar, smiling like she couldn't wait to give him an embrace.

Sydney was curious about the story behind the cane considering the woman must have been only in her early forties.

Oscar met Isabella in the middle of the path to the house, lifted her in the air, and spun her around until her cane dropped from her hand.

They laughed together and Oscar set her back down, kissing her on both cheeks. He picked up the cane from the ground and handed it to her. "Are you getting younger? You look so good."

"Gracias." Isabella glanced over at Sydney and lost her smile. "Oh. You're not . . ."

Oscar cleared his throat. "This is Sydney."

Isabella studied her from head to toe and her smile reappeared. "I'm Isabella, Oscar's sister." She waved Sydney over. "Please come here. We're from the south of Spain so the word *shy* isn't part of our vocabulary."

Oscar laughed. "So true!"

Sydney smiled and approached Isabella, kissing her on both cheeks. "A pleasure to meet you."

"The pleasure is mine." Isabella eyed Sydney's outfit and then turned to inspect her brother's. "Did you two coordinate your outfits today?"

"No."

Isabella's smile grew wider. "Serendipity!"

"Yes!" said Oscar. He stopped smiling after Sydney gave him a look. "What?" He pointed to his sister. "She said it, not me."

Ben came out from the house and hugged Oscar. "Great to see you." Then he turned to Sydney and froze. "Oh . . . hello." Ben introduced himself to Sydney and hugged her as well.

He was a tall lean man with a pale complexion and a slight British accent.

Isabella wrapped her arm around Ben's waist. "This is the love of my life even though he stabbed me in the back."

Ben laughed and kissed Isabella on the cheek. "You gave me no other choice."

"I see Sydney looks a little confused. Come inside and I'll fill you in."

Ben squeezed Oscar's shoulder. "Walk with me around the corner. I ordered Chinese takeout for lunch and we need to pick it up."

Oscar gave Sydney a wink and pointed to his sister. "You're in good hands, but don't believe anything she tells you."

Sydney smirked. "She's got an honest face."

"Smart woman," said Isabella. "Let's go in. You can help me set the table."

Sydney followed Isabella up the stairs into the house and they stopped in the first room.

"This is the family room," said Isabella. "We spend most of our time here."

She loved the hardwood floors and the antique wood-burning stove. There was an earth-tone couch with an afghan folded over the back. The room was cozy and she could picture Isabella watching movies there or reading in front of the fire.

"It's lovely."

Isabella grabbed Sydney's hand. "Speaking of lovely, tell me about this ring. You're engaged?"

Sydney shrugged and forced a smile. "Yes."

Isabella studied her for a moment. "That didn't sound like a confident yes."

"Doubts have a way of sucking the confidence out of a person."

"I agree. And you and Oscar met on the ship?"

Sydney smiled. "Fighting over an eclair."

Isabella laughed. "They're worth fighting over. And your fiancé?"

"He's working in California."

Isabella nodded. "I do find it fascinating that you and my brother are both engaged and neither of your fiancés are on the cruise with you. Do you think that's a coincidence?"

Sydney crossed her arms. "I know what you're going to say. Do you and Oscar belong to some serendipity club?"

Isabella laughed. "No, but it would be fun to start one."

She played with her silver pendant of the sun, sliding it back and forth along the silver chain on her neck.

Sydney pointed to the pendant. "That's beautiful."

"Thank you. I made it."

Sydney leaned in closer. "Really?" Isabella held it away from her neck for Sydney. "I absolutely love it." She turned it over and rubbed her thumb over the words on the back. "Carpe diem."

Sydney knew what it meant and smiled.

Isabella matched her smile. "Enjoying the magic of the moment without worrying about the future."

Sydney let out a deep breath. "I need a daily reminder of that."

"We all do."

She liked Oscar's sister. She was warm and kind. She also seemed genuinely happy and positive.

Sydney moved closer to inspect a large framed photo of a tiger on the wall. It must have been three feet wide and the tiger was close-up, looking directly at the camera. "What an amazing picture. Was this the photographer's last picture before he was eaten by the tiger?"

Isabella laughed. "That would be impossible since the photographer brought you to my home today."

Sydney gave Isabella a double take and then moved even closer to inspect the image. "Oscar took this?" Isabella nodded. "Wow. This photo looks like it should be in a magazine."

"It *was* in a Magazine. *National Geographic*. This is nothing. Follow me."

Sydney followed Isabella down the hallway to the first room and stopped at the doorway, peeking in.

"Please come in."

Sydney entered slowly and stopped. The walls of the room were filled with nature and landscape images. The ocean. The desert. The jungle. It looked like a gallery. There must have been fifty pictures taken all over the world. All framed and breathtaking.

She rubbed her forehead and stared at the pictures in awe. "Don't tell me Oscar took these photos."

"Every one of them."

She was speechless. She went around the room looking at them, becoming more and more impressed with each picture she saw.

Isabella moved closer. "I'm not surprised you didn't know. My brother has many talents but he's the most humble person I know. He was considered one of the greatest photographers of his generation—even compared to Ansel Adams."

"I don't understand. How come the press never talks about this? Whenever I watch the news or read something online they're always talking about Oscar's lifestyle or the latest woman he's going out with. Occasionally they mention an invention or something he's working on."

"First, you shouldn't believe everything you see in the news or read on the Internet. You'd be surprised how many times they get it wrong."

Oscar had said the same thing. She wondered how

many assumptions she'd made about him that weren't even true.

"Second," Isabella continued. "The press doesn't know my brother took these photos because he took them before he became famous. And he used an alias." She pointed to the signature and date at the bottom of each photo. "Martin Os."

"Why did he use an alias?"

"There was another well-known photographer named Oscar Martin who many considered one of the top master photographers in the world. Unfortunately he died and my brother didn't want any confusion between him and the other photographer, whom he admired and respected. The funny thing is I think my brother's photos are better than the other Oscar's. But that doesn't matter really. My brother did it out of the goodness of his heart. The media really has no idea how big my brother's heart is. They see he's a genius and has contributed to science and modern transportation. They see he lives a life many envy and want but they don't really know the real him. If you only knew . . ."

"I know some, but I want to know more."

Sydney could see how proud Isabella was of her brother. There was deep love and respect that she admired. She wanted to ask Isabella so many questions about Oscar. Isabella must have read her mind.

She smiled at Sydney. "Follow me and I'll tell you more."

They entered the kitchen and Isabella hung her cane

on the refrigerator door handle. She pulled four plates from the cupboard and handed them to Sydney, who promptly placed them on the placemats.

Sydney eyed the hanging cane. "Do you mind me asking you something?"

"The cane?"

Sydney smiled. "Yes. That's what I love about talking with other women. We get to the point."

Isabella laughed. "I like that part, too." She pulled four forks and four knives from the drawer and handed them to Sydney. "I fell down the stairs and suffered extensive damage to my spinal cord."

"My goodness . . ."

"Yeah. I was in bad shape. I couldn't walk."

Sydney placed the water glasses in front of each plate. "How did you recover?"

She smiled. "My brother."

"What do you mean?"

"You may have noticed he doesn't give up easily. When he wants something he's very determined."

Sydney laughed and took the pitcher of water from Isabella. "That's an understatement."

"Well, when I wasn't getting any better, Oscar told me to not give up. He spent hours, days, weeks, researching alternative medicine and breakthrough procedures from doctors and research labs all over the world. Then, finally, he was confident he had found someone who he thought could help me."

"Where did he find him?"

"In London, at the Institute of Neurology. But the procedure was outrageously expensive, so my brother gave up his photography and sold hundreds of patents to an aeronautics company in California that designed transportation of the future. Then he joined their team to help bring some of his inventions to life. He came up with most of the ideas while he was attending Stanford. He raised millions for my procedure. Then when my rehabilitation bills started getting a little crazy, he sold more patents and paid them off. He put his entire life, his passion, on hold for me."

"He doesn't like inventing things? Isn't that his passion?"

"He doesn't really talk about it much, but he can come up with those ideas without really putting in an effort. But he says it hurts his brain to concentrate so much. He prefers photography because it's almost a form of relaxation for him. He stopped doing it for me. He's the reason I'm walking today."

Sydney was happy for Isabella but felt bad for judging Oscar. He'd sacrificed his life and his passion for his sister. It was obvious he'd do anything for her. And he had.

"So he flew you to London?"

"First class. Oscar was there through all the consultations, the tests, and for the cell transplant."

"What did they do that other doctors couldn't?"

"This will sound strange, because it sounded strange to me when they told me what they wanted to do. They removed cells from my nasal cavity, grew them in a culture, and then injected them into my spinal cord above and below where I had the damage."

Sydney shook her head. "How do they think of these things? And *who* thought of it? That's what amazes me the most."

"Professor Benjamin Nicholls, a Brit."

Sydney blinked. "Wait. Benjamin Nicholls . . . You don't mean *your* Ben, do you?"

Isabella smiled and nodded.

Sydney's entire body was covered in goose bumps. "You mean to tell me that you ended up marrying the person who helped you walk again?"

Isabella nodded again. "Serendipity!"

Sydney's eyes stung and she felt moisture coming on. "I'm not going to cry. No, no, no . . ."

Too late. The tears came.

"Ahhh," said Isabella. "You're so sweet. You don't have to cry for me."

"These are happy tears! Your story is so beautiful!"

Isabella leaned forward and hugged Sydney. "Thank you. I happen to agree with you." She rubbed Sydney's back. "I like you. I can see you have a good heart."

Sydney wiped her eyes. "Thanks. You, too."

They hugged again as Oscar and Ben returned with the Chinese food.

Oscar froze. "This doesn't look good."

Sydney walked directly over to Oscar and hugged him. "You're a good man." Then she turned and hugged Ben. "You, too. Thank you."

Oscar pulled the food containers from the bag and set them on the counter. "Do I want to know what you talked about while we were gone?"

Isabella opened one of the containers. "No, you don't."

He wagged his finger at his sister. "I'm guessing confidential information was leaked."

"I'm too proud of you not to tell the world how wonderful you are. You know that."

"That's fine, but you will now suffer the consequences." He grabbed the box of chow mein from her and held it close to his body. "No food for you!"

Sydney laughed. "Nice try. Your secret is out."

CHAPTER ELEVEN

Oscar smiled as he watched Sydney chat with his sister. He hadn't been gone that long and they had already bonded. You'd think they had known each other for years. It was fascinating to watch since Isabella hadn't approved of any of the women in the past.

None of them.

Isabella had always said she could tell when a woman didn't have enough love in her heart. She obviously approved of Sydney, but why should that be a surprise? He approved of her, too. In fact, there no doubt in his mind that he wanted Sydney in his life. His feelings got stronger every minute he spent with her. Every second.

As for his sister, how could he not love that proud look on her face? She was his biggest fan. She said she'd never forget what he'd done but he was sure most people would have done the same thing if they were in his shoes. They were family. Nothing was more important than that. Still, he wondered *how* much she'd told Sydney. Based on the look on Sydney's face he would guess everything.

Isabella handed Oscar a bottle of wine. "Could you open this for me? I hadn't planned on it, but I have suddenly changed my mind." She winked at Sydney. "And please, let's all sit and eat while the food is hot. Don't be shy, Sydney."

Oscar opened the wine bottle and poured four glasses.

Sydney held her glass out over the table and giggled. "To serendipity."

"Yes!" said Isabella.

Oscar raised an eyebrow. "Wait a minute. You're toasting serendipity?"

"You've got a problem with that?"

"Of course not, I'm just . . . surprised."

"Can't a person have a change of heart?"

"Absolutely, but what brought on this sudden change?"

"I admit I've had my doubts in the past but I'm starting to see the light. The way Isabella and Ben met was not a coincidence."

"And the way you and my brother met," said Isabella.

Oscar glanced back over at Sydney, who appeared to be blushing.

Thirty minutes later, after non-stop conversation and laughter, they had finished lunch.

Sydney turned to Ben and smiled. "How did you two end up here in Victoria? It's so far away from London and doesn't seem like a typical place for people to relocate to."

"You'd be surprised," said Ben. "Over fifty percent of

the population in British Columbia is from England and Scotland. But to answer your question, I was recruited to head up the research staff at the University of British Columbia, Faculty of Medicine. It was a prestigious position I just couldn't pass up and it was an easy decision since moving here put Isabella closer to Oscar."

Sydney smiled. "That's so sweet. So, you still work at the university?"

"No. Five years later I started my own consulting firm specializing in neurophysiology. I travel quite a bit, so I hired Isabella as my assistant." He smiled. "Now I can take her with me."

"That's wonderful. Sounds like we have a lot in common. I love to travel, too."

Isabella reached over and placed her hand on top of her brother's. "So does Oscar."

Oscar began to stand up. "That deserves another hug, no?"

Sydney laughed and pushed him back down. She grabbed the fortune cookies. "I'll distract you with these." She handed one to each of them. "Let's see what life has in store for us. Isabella, you go first."

"Okay." She snapped her fortune cookie in half, pulled the piece of paper out, and read it. "Someone special will visit you soon." She winced. "Wait a minute, this already happened. I don't like this fortune at all. Can I have another one?"

Ben broke open his fortune cookie and popped a piece in his mouth. "Sorry, one per person. Maybe mine will make up for it." He winked at Isabella and held his fortune close to his eyes, so he could read it. "Your wife will prepare your favorite scones for you today."

Isabella laughed and tried to reach over and grab the fortune from Ben. "Give me that. I want to see."

He held it out of her reach. "You don't need to see it. It says it right here! Get cooking!"

"*You* should make *me* scones."

He leaned over and kissed her. "Whatever you wish, my love."

Sydney sighed and pointed to Oscar. "Okay, your turn."

"You first."

"No, you first."

"I insist."

"*I* insist."

Oscar stared at her. "You can't insist after I insist. I was first."

"You *were* first which means my *insist* cancels out *your* insist."

"How does yours cancel out mine?"

"It just does."

Oscar picked up the fortune cookie from the table. "You win this time."

Sydney smirked. "I always win."

Isabella laughed. "You two act like an old married couple. It's fascinating considering you just met."

Oscar and Sydney locked eyes for a few moments and then Sydney played with her fortune cookie.

If this is what an old married couple felt like, Oscar was in. He enjoyed the playful banter with Sydney. He snapped the fortune cookie in half and read it. "Be careful of the treacherous ways of a certain feisty California woman."

Sydney laughed and smacked him on the arm. "What is it with you men? You forgot how to read?"

Oscar laughed and pointed to the fortune. "That's what it says!"

Ben held up his fortune and tried to keep a straight face. "I read mine correctly, too. Scones!"

Oscar held his hand out toward Ben. "Since the ladies don't believe you, I would be happy to confirm your fortune."

Ben handed him the piece of paper. "That's so kind of you."

"It's a true pleasure." Oscar analyzed it and nodded. "It's true. Scones with a capital S!"

The four of them shared a laugh as Isabella stood to clear some things from the table. "I have an idea. Since my husband here is in the mood for scones and I'm in *no* mood to make them, how about we go for a nice walk and have afternoon tea and scones at The Empress Hotel?"

Ben stood. "Great idea! I'll help clean up."

"Wait!" said Sydney, holding up her fortune cookie. "What about me?"

"Oh!" said Isabella, sitting back down. "Ben, wait. Sorry, Sydney. Please read your fortune."

"Thank you." She broke her cookie in half and pulled

out the fortune. She cleared her throat and read it. "You have—" She cleared her throat again and stared at the fortune for a moment. She glanced around the table at the six eyes intensely focused on her.

Isabella moved up on the edge of her seat. "What? Please continue."

"Uh . . ."

Oscar could see Sydney's face changing colors. It almost matched her hair. What did her fortune say? If it had something to do with love, hopefully it involved him. Most people didn't believe in those fortunes but it was crazy how sometimes they just seem to fit. He had to know what it said.

He reached over and plucked the fortune from Sydney's hands. "It would be a pleasure to read it for you."

"No!" Sydney stood and lunged for the fortune. She lost her balance and fell over the top of Oscar's lap.

Oscar looked down at the most beautiful bottom staring right back up at him. "Please, make yourself comfortable. And take your time getting up because I'm enjoying the view."

She pushed herself off Oscar. "Sorry." She smoothed out her skirt and pointed to the fortune in his hand. "You might as well read it now."

Oscar raised the piece of paper and read. "You have met your perfect match." He grinned. "I like this one for some reason."

"How about that afternoon tea?" Sydney looked

toward the hallway. "May I use the restroom before we go?"

Isabella stood. "Of course. First door on the left."

Oscar peeked around the corner to make sure Sydney was inside the bathroom and then approached his sister. "What do you think of Sydney?"

Isabella smiled. "I adore her. She's beautiful, kind, funny . . . And, most importantly, she has a good heart. There's something so strong between you two. I know you and I saw it in her."

"It's crazy, isn't it?"

"Crazy and wonderful. But you have a situation on your hands. Sydney is an amazing woman, but you're engaged to someone else. Do you know what you're going to do?"

He looked back toward the bathroom and then leaned into Isabella, keeping his voice low. "I'm not marrying Alexa. I'll tell her as soon as I get back."

Isabella jumped and hugged Oscar. "Yes!"

He put his finger to his lips. "Shhh!" Oscar chuckled. "Glad you approve of my decision."

"That woman wasn't good enough for you. What about Sydney?"

"I don't know yet, but I have high hopes." He smiled. "The only thing I can do is follow my heart and see where it takes me."

She patted him on the chest. "That's the only way."

∽

Sydney walked with Isabella, Ben, and Oscar toward The Empress Hotel for afternoon tea. It was gorgeous outside, but her mind wasn't on the weather. She replayed that ridiculous scene where she ended up on Oscar's lap over and over again in her head.

What was she thinking?

Isabella reached over and rubbed the side of Sydney's arm. "Relax. It's okay."

She was right. Sydney needed to clear her mind. A red double-decker tourist bus came in their direction and Sydney smiled.

Isabella led them across the football field-sized lawn of the BC Parliament Buildings. She glanced over at the Romanesque-style architecture with the large dome in the middle. The buildings reminded her a little bit of San Francisco City Hall.

Great. Now she was thinking about home. The place where she had an unfulfilling job.

And a fiancé. Neither of which she wanted any longer.

She had serious doubts about marrying Elliot. He was a kind man, but they had different goals in life. She didn't have a problem that he worked so much. He enjoyed his job in sales. The problem was his job was a higher priority than she was.

She glanced over at Oscar wondering what was going on in his mind. He'd avoided the topic of his fiancée, but it would have to be addressed soon.

Hundreds of people were scattered across the lawn, reading and relaxing. Maybe once she had a cup of tea in her hands she'd be able to clear her mind and settle down. They crossed the street toward the inner harbor and walked along the water, stopping occasionally to watch a street entertainer or peek at something for sale at one of the kiosks. Then they crossed the street and entered The Empress Hotel.

"Right this way," said the hostess.

They followed her through the tea lobby and past the pianist toward their table.

She was amazed how many people were there. "People really like to drink tea in Victoria."

The hostess smiled. "It's been a tradition here at the hotel for over a century."

"I love it." Sydney eyed the antique tapestries, rugs, and vintage furnishings as she walked next to Oscar. "The city and hotel are very European."

"Now you know why so many Europeans are here," said Ben. "It's a wonderful place to live and it's like we still have a little bit of home all around us."

Oscar pointed to a portrait on the wall. "King George V and his wife, Queen Mary. Royalty, celebrities, and dignitaries from all over the world have enjoyed afternoon tea here."

"Very true, Mr. Martin." The hostess gestured to their table. "In fact, you'll be seated here at what we affectionately call the John Travolta Table."

Isabella lit up and ran her fingers along the hand-carved table. "I've got chills . . ."

Sydney laughed. "They're multiplying!"

"*Grease* is one of my favorite movies."

"Mine, too!"

Oscar smiled and pulled out one of the elegant wingback chairs for Sydney. "Why do I have this suspicion that the two of you will stay in touch after today?"

Sydney sat and placed a hand on top of Isabella's. "Of course we will. Your sister is wonderful."

Isabella patted the top of her hand. "Thank you. You, too. And I have so many other secrets about my brother I still need to share with you."

Oscar waved a finger at her. "This is not necessary. I'll lose all of my superpowers without my secrets."

Sydney shook her head. "On the contrary. The more I learn about you, the more I like you."

Did she really just say that? Was it getting warm in there?

"This I like to hear, Miss St. James."

"Well, you can just forget you heard that. I wasn't supposed to say that out loud." She turned away, pretending to be dramatic.

The girls laughed as the waiter approached. "Welcome to Afternoon Tea, Mr. Martin. Nice to have you back."

"Thank you."

The white-haired waiter in the black tuxedo smiled and turned to Sydney. "Your first time?"

"It's that obvious?"

He chuckled. "The eyes wide-open are usually a dead giveaway. I've been an employee here for almost forty years. I know things even the owner of the hotel doesn't know!"

"That's amazing. Were you working the day John Travolta came in?"

"Yes, ma'am. I served him right at this table. I've also had the pleasure of serving Barbra Streisand and Mel Gibson. I'll be right back with your tea and an assortment of pastries and scones."

Ben sat up. "Scones! The fortune was right!"

The four of them laughed and chatted until the waiter returned ten minutes later.

He commenced with the sterling silver service and smiled. "We serve over five hundred thousand cups of tea every year!"

Sydney admired the proud look on the waiter's face. He loved his job, which was wonderful to see. She was tired of her job and the constant stress, but she shouldn't be thinking about that.

Isabella added milk and sugar to her tea and took a sip. "Sydney, what do you do for a living?"

Oscar's sister was a mind reader.

"I'm an administrative assistant. Although lately I've had thoughts of quitting and going back to what I did before."

"Which was?"

"I had a travel blog. I traveled and wrote about it. I absolutely loved it."

"You can get paid for that?"

"Yes, but the business needs to be built up to get a steady stream of advertisers."

She nodded and then her eyes grew. "Wouldn't it be amazing if you and Oscar ended up working together? You write about travel and he takes his wonderful photos? You could even publish travel books."

Ben reached over and grabbed a vanilla scone. "Great idea."

That would be amazing, indeed. She would sign up for that in a heartbeat.

"I've been thinking about the same thing," said Oscar. "Going back to photography. It's what I love to do and I've missed it." He glanced at Sydney. "It was wonderful to be shooting again. Thanks to you, I've got that passion back."

Sydney shrugged. "I doubt the passion was ever gone. You just had things going on and it was pushed to the side."

"I'll be eternally grateful for what you've done."

They locked gazes and then Sydney reached for a blueberry pastry.

Oscar turned to Isabella. "Watch out for Sydney. She pretends to innocently grab the dessert, but I know from firsthand experience that she'll attack you with it when you least expect it."

Sydney lifted the pastry. "Don't tempt me."

Oscar leaned away in his chair and laughed.

For the next twenty minutes they sipped on tea and ate too many scones and pastries. The pianist started a new song, "L-O-V-E" by Nat King Cole.

Sydney swayed back and forth in her seat and hummed along. "I love this song."

Oscar stood and held out his hand. "Please come with me. I would like to show you something."

Sydney stared at his hand for a moment and then took it. She stood and Oscar led her through the tea lobby. They were holding hands and it was wonderful. Her pulse pounded in her ears. She was sure something memorable was about to happen. Something she would never forget.

"Where are we going?" she asked, hoping to get a clue.

He grinned. "You'll see in a moment. Almost there."

He walked toward the double doors with the sign overhead.

Crystal Ballroom.

Were they going inside? She had no idea what he was up to.

Oscar looked around as if he were going to enter illegally. Then he reached for the handle, pulling the door open. He guided Sydney through to enter the ballroom before him and then he let the door close behind him. They took a few steps into the room and stopped, looking around.

Oscar chuckled. "I admit this is not what I was expecting."

She stared up at the countless chandeliers in the room. Now she knew how the Crystal Ballroom got its name. The room was decorated for a wedding, one that would most likely take place later in the evening. She glanced around the room at the tables covered in lavender linens that matched their outfits.

Oscar turned and looked at Sydney's lavender top and then down at his own lavender shirt.

She held up her hand. "Don't say it."

"I wasn't going to say anything."

"Right."

The tables were set with silver, china, and champagne glasses. The tall glass cylinder centerpieces were filled with ivory roses and white hydrangeas.

Oscar walked to the center of the dance floor and spun around. "Around a hundred years ago . . . Edward, Prince of Wales, danced in this very spot. A waltz."

"And you know how to waltz?"

He shook his head. "Not a clue."

She chuckled, but cut herself off when he held his hand out in her direction.

"There's no music," she said.

"We'll make our own."

He had to say something like that.

She swallowed hard, but maintained eye contact with him. "Okay . . ."

He grinned and wiggled the fingers of his extended hand, waiting for her. "I've got you under my skin."

Her legs felt weak. Hopefully, he would catch her when she passed out.

He raised an eyebrow. "Do you know the song?"

"What song?"

He chuckled. "Are you paying attention?"

"I'm having great difficulty . . ."

"There's a classic song called 'I've Got You Under My Skin.' Do you know it?"

She nodded.

"Good. Think of that song while we dance. I'm not going to sing because I don't want to do a disservice to it. Please take my hand."

He was serious. There went her heart rate again, deciding to test the speed limit. She hesitated, but then moved slowly in Oscar's direction. His eyes were intense. He didn't blink. All their conversations, all their disagreements, all their playing around was about to fly out the window. This moment they would experience pure, raw emotion. She was sure of it. And there was nothing more she wanted than this. No more fighting it. No more excuses.

She slid her hand into his and held his gaze. He inched closer. His other hand traveled from her waist to the small of her back. He pulled her closer, not saying a word. Their bodies were so connected. The heat through his clothes was intense, as if they were naked.

She pulled away and shook her head. "My heart is about to explode out of my chest."

"Not before mine."

She loved that he was nervous, too. They were moving into new territory here.

He eyed her lips for a moment, but didn't go for the kiss.

Why was he waiting? It was the perfect time for a kiss.

Instead, he pulled her even closer and placed his cheek against hers. Then they danced.

She wasn't going to complain. It was wonderful.

She closed her eyes as they swayed back and forth. He was right. They were making their own music. Her imagination took off and she pictured this as their wedding day.

Their first dance.

But there was one thing she needed to do before this went any further.

She pulled away again and stared at him for a few moments. "Oscar . . ."

"Yes . . ."

She broke eye contact with him, gazing down to her hand. She spun the engagement ring around her finger a few times, deep in thought. Then she slid the ring off her finger and clutched it in the palm of her hand.

Much better.

Oscar's eyes opened wider. He raised his gaze from her hand, back to her eyes. Then he looked at her lips.

He was going to drive her crazy if he didn't kiss her immediately. She eyed his lips, hoping that would give him the hint to—

His lips were on hers. First gentle, then she let him in for something deeper, more passionate.

Too passionate. She didn't think she could handle it. Was she going to pass out?

She pulled away.

"What is it?" he asked.

Her heavy breath continued. "This is too much."

"I was just warming up."

She laughed. "You're going to kill me with your kisses."

"Not a bad way to die . . ."

Their eyes were locked as he stepped closer again. Then he went in for another kiss. Even better than the first kiss.

After a few seconds he smiled and spun her around. "You make me a happy man."

"You make me a happy woman. And that kiss . . ."

"Yes. That kiss." He pulled her body against his again and caressed the side of her cheek. "It was beautiful. Magical . . ."

"I agree."

"And?"

"Do that to me one more time."

He grinned. "Just one more time?"

"For now."

CHAPTER TWELVE

Sydney awoke the next morning and turned to her side, checking on Gina. Her best friend was still asleep. She got out of bed and tiptoed to the bathroom. Gina had gotten in later than Sydney so she must have been pretty tired. After she finished in the bathroom she came back out into the cabin and moved the curtain over, peeking out of the porthole. It would be their last day at sea. If she had to guess she'd say they were somewhere off the coast of Washington or Oregon. Tomorrow they'd be back in San Francisco where she would have to do something she didn't look forward to doing.

Break up with Elliot.

Gina yawned. "Hey, hon. Go ahead, open the curtain."

"Okay." Sydney slid the curtain open, letting a little light into the cabin. She sat on the bed next to Gina and rubbed her leg through the blanket. "I was surprised you weren't here when I got in last night. What time did you get in?"

"About twenty minutes after my third margarita."

Sydney laughed. "You do remember what you did, though?"

"Of course. Unlike some people I know I can hold my liquor just fine, thank you very much."

That was the truth. In college Gina used to compete in drinking games against the guys and usually won. Sydney, on the other hand, could barely make it through one drink before feeling a little loopy.

Gina sat up in bed. "Leo gave me a private tour of the ship. It's crazy what they do behind the scenes!"

"You had a good time?"

"A great time. Leo is yummy." She moaned and smiled. "What about you? Tell me about Victoria. Anything exciting happen?"

Sydney hesitated and then held up her ring finger. "This happened."

Gina gasped and threw her hand over her mouth. "No! What did you do with your engagement ring? You lost it?"

"No." Sydney circled around the bed and pulled open the nightstand drawer. She grabbed the engagement ring from inside and held it up. "I have it right here. And I can't marry Elliot."

"You're crazy."

"Quite possibly."

"What happened yesterday?"

"Everything. It was an amazing day. Just wonderful. Oscar is . . ."

"Oscar is Oscar. Every woman in the world wants to be with him."

"Yeah . . ."

Gina pointed to Sydney's face. "Your eyes sparkle when you talk about him. Wow. You're falling in love with Oscar Martin."

She smiled. "Maybe."

"Sydney! I really like Oscar and think he's a cool guy, but are you one hundred percent certain about him? He has his reputation, you know. Did he ask you back to his suite last night?"

"No. He never mentioned sex, going back to his suite, or anything close to that. He was a perfect gentleman."

"Are you sure you know what you're doing? You're over Elliot?"

"Yes. Absolutely. Even if I didn't end up with Oscar, it's clear I shouldn't be with Elliot. I know he's a good man. But I've had a taste of true passion and I want more of that! You should see the way Oscar looks at me."

"Oh, I've seen it."

"Elliot never looked at me that way. Elliot doesn't like to dance. He doesn't like to travel. And he definitely doesn't kiss with passion like Oscar does."

"Did he tell you he was calling off his own wedding?"

He hadn't. Sydney had been so caught up in the romance of the day that the subject never came up.

"Aha!" said Gina, moving closer. "I need to talk with him."

"No!" Sydney threw a pillow at Gina.

"Yes. I need to test him. Make sure he isn't playing you."

"Please. He's not a player."

"If you're so confident then you won't mind playing along. Just a little test to make sure he's sincere. Humor me."

A test wasn't necessary, but Sydney had to admit she'd feel better if Oscar told her he wasn't going through with his wedding. He'd never mentioned it. And as crazy as it sounded, she was falling in love with him. She could picture them together. Forever. Now she just needed to hear that from him.

Sydney stood and grabbed her jeans from the top of the dresser. "Fine. Let's go eat breakfast. Oscar will be there in five minutes, but please take it easy on the guy. He's not who you think he is."

Gina smiled. "I'll be the judge of that."

Oscar had more energy this morning than he'd had in years. He sang in the shower. He sang as he got dressed. He whistled as he left the suite. All because of Sydney. Yesterday had been the perfect day. The lunch. The tea. The dance. The kiss.

Oscar and Sydney had something special and she'd

confirmed it when she slid the engagement ring off her finger. He'd been ready to settle down and have a family the last couple of years. Then he'd met Alexa and thought she'd be a good choice. But you don't choose the people you want to love. You can't force it. Love finds you. And it happens on its own and when it's ready.

He felt so many things for Sydney. Crazy, considering they'd met a little over a week ago when she had smashed that eclair in his face. He smiled just thinking about it. What a woman. But they still had a lot to talk about. Their relationship. Their future. Because they definitely had a future.

He waited outside of the restaurant and checked his watch. Sydney had said she would most likely see him around ten for breakfast.

He smiled when he felt the tug on his arm and turned around. Then he raised an eyebrow. "Hello, Gina. How are you on this beautiful—"

"Come with me." Gina pulled Oscar toward The Sweet Tooth Cafe. "We need to talk."

"I like to talk." He used his free arm to point to the cafe. "Is Sydney inside?"

"Yes. I wanted to talk to you alone, but she wouldn't let me. She said she wanted to make sure there were witnesses in case I tried to kill you."

"Ahh . . ."

That was cute. Gina was being protective of her best friend and he didn't blame her one bit. He'd do the same for any of his friends. Obviously, Sydney had told her the story of what happened yesterday and she was intervening. It didn't worry Oscar. Even if she didn't approve of what was happening and tried to stop it, she wouldn't be able to.

Love always wins.

She continued to drag Oscar into the cafe and into the line. "Order coffee and join us over there." She pointed to the table underneath the picture of Sumatra coffee beans where Sydney sat with her coffee and food. "If you try to escape I swear I'll hunt you down and throw you overboard."

He grinned. "My sister gets the same way when she doesn't have food in her system. Start eating and I'll be right there."

She gave him a look and he laughed inside. He ordered an espresso and waited for the barista to prepare it. When it was ready, he grabbed it and scanned the breakfast pastry display. He chose a croissant and approached Gina and Sydney's table.

This would be fun.

He stopped in front of their table and glanced at Gina. "Should I have my lawyer present?"

Sydney snorted.

Gina gave him the death stare. "Sit."

"Of course." He pulled the chair out and sat, eyeing Sydney's hand. No ring. Good. She hadn't had second thoughts.

"Always a pleasure to see you, Miss St. James. No eclairs today?"

She finished chewing a bite of her bagel with cream

cheese and smiled. "I asked, but they only have them in the evenings. Mostly breakfast items in the morning."

"I consider the eclair a twenty-four-hour food item."

She smiled. "Me, too."

They locked gazes for a moment and he was suddenly transported back to the dance floor yesterday at The Empress Hotel. Holding her in his arms and kissing her. It took his breath away. Never before had he been so captivated by a woman.

Gina smacked him on the arm. "Wake up, Romeo, and pay attention. Take your eyes off of my friend's lips because we need to talk. Seriously."

Sydney looked like she wanted to laugh, but did a great job of keeping a semi-straight face. She kept quiet, but her eyes were talking to him. He enjoyed what they were saying.

Gina could go on all day long about how she thought this was a mistake, but it wouldn't matter. His mind was made up. He wanted Sydney. Forever.

He sat up straight and prepared for the interrogation. "I'm ready when you are. Call your first witness."

Sydney burst out laughing. Her laughter was so contagious that Oscar found himself laughing with her. So much for holding it together.

Gina wrinkled her nose. "This is not funny." She gestured to Sydney. "This is my best friend and I'm worried about her. You're engaged to be married, Oscar. So I'd like to know what do you think you're doing?"

He thought about her question and took a sip of his espresso. "I'm falling in love with your best friend."

Gina stared at him for a few seconds. "Okay . . ."

Maybe she didn't expect honesty, but she seemed to be a little surprised by his answer. So did Sydney, who sat up straight, eyes bright and open in Oscar's direction. She licked her lips.

"Please don't do that," said Oscar. "It's a distraction and I need to have a clear mind for this interrogation."

"Oscar . . ."

"Yes, Gina . . ."

"Are you still getting married?"

"To whom?"

"To Alexa," she said a little too loudly.

Oscar glanced around the cafe and then scooted in closer to Gina. "I appreciate your concern about Sydney and I don't mind having this conversation with you, but please keep it down. The press is everywhere and I don't want this story to leak. I have no intention of marrying Alexa. And out of respect for her I want to tell her personally when I get home. It'll be the first thing I say when I walk through the door. I mean, after I say hello, of course. And you and I both know Sydney's plans since she's no longer wearing a certain ring on a certain finger."

"And?"

"And . . . what?"

"What do you intend to do after you call off your wedding?"

He grinned. "Besides kiss Sydney every day and every night?"

Sydney perked up. "Great answer."

Gina held up a finger. "Eat your bagel and be quiet. Oscar, please. I need to know your plan."

"Honestly, we haven't come up with a plan yet. Sydney and I didn't plan any of this. This was serendipity."

"Serendipity . . ."

"Yes."

"Sydney doesn't believe in serendipity."

He grinned. "She does now."

Gina cranked her head toward Sydney. "Is this true?"

Sydney took a sip of her coffee. "Guilty as charged, your honor." She giggled and took another bite of her bagel.

"Anyway," continued Oscar, winking at Sydney. "My life will go through some radical changes over the next few weeks. Personally and professionally. I'm seeing things much more clearly now, thanks to Sydney. All I can say is you'll have to trust your best friend to make the right decision. That beautiful, feisty woman is also intelligent. She knows what she's doing."

Sydney set the bagel down on her plate and wiped her mouth with the napkin. "There's that word again . . ."

"Intelligent?"

"Feisty."

Oscar nodded. "It fits, but if you prefer, I can call you spirited or spunky."

"Let's stick with feisty."

"You see how easy this is? We're making life's important decisions together."

Gina sighed. "Important decisions? Whether or not she wants to be called feisty? Come on—this is weird. Why are you both so calm? I'd be freaking out right now if I were in either of your shoes!"

Sydney smiled. "You're freaking out without being in our shoes."

Oscar reached over and placed a hand on top of Gina's. "Sydney is lucky to have a friend as wonderful and caring as you." Gina glanced down at his hand as he continued. "I have to cut this short, but I look forward to getting to know you better." He winked at Gina, stood, and turned to Sydney. "Since this is our last full day at sea, Leo has lined up interviews for me most of the day . . . television, radio, newspaper, etcetera. I won't bore you with the details, but before I go I would like to invite you to join me in my suite at 8:28 PM this evening."

Sydney laughed. "What's happening at 8:28 PM?"

"The sunset."

"Oh . . ."

"I would like to experience it with you on my balcony and also share a toast."

"That sounds wonderful. Can I come casual?"

"As casual as you want."

"Great. What will we be toasting?"

"I'll give you a hint. It starts with an S and ends in *erendipity*."

Gina sighed. "You two are disgusting."

Oscar needed a shot of espresso, or even better, a glimpse of lovely Sydney. The sight of her gave him an overload of energy and he needed it right now. He'd already conducted seven interviews and had one left.

Fortunately, the last interview would be in his suite instead of the Polar Lounge where the others had taken place. He changed his clothes in the loft so he didn't appear to be wearing the same thing for every interview. At the sound of the doorbell he went downstairs to let the television crew in. He was surprised when it was Leo.

Leo slapped Oscar on the arm and flew past him into the suite. "Change of plans. Unfortunately, the last interview you had with The Travel Channel isn't going to happen."

Oscar didn't have a problem with that. "Any particular reason or they just changed their minds?"

"They're pissed off, unfortunately. The interview you did for Channel Seven this morning was transmitted via satellite and aired an hour ago in San Francisco. Plus, their network picked it up and aired it nationally thirty minutes after the local story ran. The Travel Channel was promised they would be the first to air your story on a new show about cruises but Channel Seven says they never got the memo. That's a lot of publicity down the drain since it was an interview that would have aired internationally. Totally sucks."

This loss of publicity could cost the company revenue. Millions. Not good when you're starting out. Oscar was sure he could help. "I have an idea."

"Hit me with it."

"How about if I give them an exclusive interview and talk about things I didn't mention in any of the other interviews? What if I mentioned how I met my future wife on this cruise?"

Leo's eyes got wider. "Seriously? You see yourself marrying Sydney?"

"Absolutely. Of course, we have many things to talk about but I see it very clearly."

"That's amazing. And how would she feel about the interview?"

"I think she'd be okay with it, but I wouldn't do it without her approval. And The Travel Channel would have to wait until everything is in place—most likely weeks or months from now. But if it helps you, I'll do it."

Leo hugged Oscar. "You're the best. Thank you."

"Anything for you."

Thirty minutes after Leo had left, Oscar ordered two gin fizzes from room service. After they arrived he took them outside to the balcony and placed them on the bar. Five minutes later, he opened the door for Sydney.

She stepped inside his suite and he slowly closed the door behind her. Even in what she considered casual clothes—blue jeans and a sunny yellow blouse—she was stunning.

He stepped forward and kissed her on both cheeks. In Spain you typically wouldn't repeat this greeting, but he wasn't even close to finished. He kissed her left cheek again and on the way back over to the right one he accidentally brushed her lips with his on purpose. She moaned, which signaled his brain to kiss her on the lips. He pulled her close and she ran her hands up his chest to their final resting place around his neck.

The kiss in The Empress Hotel was spectacular, but this one passed it like it was standing still. He pulled away slowly and gazed into her eyes. "This is real."

"Yes . . ."

He took a deep breath and sighed. "I could continue doing that for hours, days even, but that could lead to other things and . . . I don't think it would be appropriate until you and I take care of things when we get home. You understand?"

She smiled. "Yes. I agree."

"Good." He kissed her on the lips. Then he kissed her again. And again. He pulled away and chuckled. "I need to stop doing that. Let's go to the balcony." He took her hand and led her through the suite to the open sliding glass door. They stepped outside and made their way to the edge of the balcony. The sun was about to set—maybe just another few minutes.

He held up his finger. "Almost forgot . . ." He took a few steps toward the outdoor bar and grabbed the two

AN ECLAIR TO REMEMBER 159

drinks from the counter. He turned and handed one of them to her.

She smiled. "Gin fizz?"

He nodded and held his glass out. "To serendipity. To us."

She clinked his glass. "Cheers." She took a sip and turned toward the sunset. "We need a selfie." She pulled her smartphone from her purse.

"No, no . . ."

"Why not?"

Oscar pointed to the side of the outdoor dining table where his camera was setup on a tripod and ready to go. He held up a remote control for the camera and grinned.

"Look at you!" she laughed. "That's what I love to see. A man who is prepared." She set her purse down on the table and Oscar snapped a few pictures of them with the sunset directly between their heads.

They sat on one of the lounge chairs and Sydney cuddled up against Oscar. They talked over two hours about life, family, and dreams. They discovered even more how aligned their goals and desires were.

He grinned. "You and I make a great team, you know that?"

"Yes."

"We should seriously look at the possibility of working together as well. You haven't been satisfied with your job and should get back to what you're passionate about. I need to do the same."

"What did you have in mind?"

"Just like Isabella said. It would be amazing if you wrote about travel and I documented it with photos. There are so many possibilities . . . a website, a blog, a magazine, publishing travel books. Imagine, traveling the world and doing what we love."

She smiled. "That would be a dream."

He grinned. "We can make that dream a reality." He grabbed her hand and began massaging it.

"Wow . . ." She closed her eyes and signed. "You should probably stop doing that." If it continued much longer she would tear his clothes off and they had agreed to wait. She pulled her hand out from between his smooth, sexy fingers. "Is that what you were doing to Gina in the lounge that night?"

He chuckled. "Yes. But you were too stubborn to let me do it to you."

"Not stubborn. Scared . . ."

"Like when you got the fortune about meeting your perfect match. You were scared because it might be true?"

"Yes. And because I *hoped* it was true."

"It is true. You've met your perfect match. And so have I."

CHAPTER THIRTEEN

Sydney leaned against the rail on the Sky View Deck of the ship and stared out at the San Francisco Bay. Her eyes traveled from Angel Island to Sausalito and the Golden Gate Bridge. Soon she would disembark and head back to reality. That's not to say that what had happened on her vacation hadn't been reality, but she now had a list of things she had to get done. Breaking up with Elliot was at the top.

She also had to decide the fate of her job. She had been unfulfilled and couldn't continue to live that way for much longer. Oscar's idea of working together as a team sounded amazing, but she wouldn't quit her job until she knew it was a definite plan. And she had enough in her savings as emergency backup in case Oscar's idea didn't take off immediately.

Sydney and Oscar. Oscar and Sydney. It had a nice ring to it.

Nerves built up in the pit of her stomach. She took a deep breath of the cool morning air, hoping to blow away some of that anxiety. Too bad it didn't work.

Oscar would be there any minute to say goodbye. They had agreed last night to meet on the Sky View Deck to keep their goodbyes brief. They would also discuss the plan on when they would see each other next. She would have to find a new place to live since she had been living with Elliot. The move wouldn't be too difficult though, since most of the furniture was Elliot's. She had ended up selling most of her stuff before she had moved in with him.

Would she move in with Oscar? Fortunately, Gina had said she could stay with her as long as she wanted. She apologized to Gina many times for not being around to do things with her on the vacation but Gina had had such an amazing night with Leo that she didn't even care. She loved that those two hit it off. Maybe they could have a double wedding. She laughed at the idea.

She loved when Oscar talked about serendipity. He was so passionate about it, which was rare for a man. Just the thought brought a smile to her face.

"There's that beautiful smile that I love," said Oscar, approaching. "How did you sleep?"

Sydney crinkled her nose. "Not so well."

"Me, neither. Lots on the mind."

She nodded and looked around. "Funny how there's nobody up here now. Remember how crazy it was when we cruised through Glacier Bay?"

"Yes." He gestured to the beautiful bay in front of

them. "Even though this bay is beautiful, the passengers have probably seen it many times since most of them live nearby. I guess they take it for granted now."

Funny how both of them were avoiding the topic that they should really be discussing . . . the future.

Maybe he was just as nervous as she was.

He rubbed her arm. "You okay?"

She shrugged. "Nerves."

"Ahh." He grinned. "Glad I'm not the only one." They were quiet for a few moments, staring out at the bay. Oscar pointed to the Golden Gate Bridge. "My favorite bridge. Have you ever walked across it?"

She stared at it and blinked. "No."

"Don't tell me this! You're a native Californian. Did you know people travel from all over the world just to see it and walk across it?"

"Well, I knew the bridge was one of the popular tourist destinations in the country, but I didn't know about the walking across part."

"Even with the noise of thousands of cars passing by, it's exhilarating. It's a great way to clear your head when you've got too much going on up there."

Sydney let out a nervous laugh. "Maybe I should get off the ship and go straight there. I could use it."

Oscar chuckled. "You'll be fine, but you have to walk across it in the future. The view from the middle of the bridge is breathtaking. In fact, you and I will do it one day."

She smiled. "I'd like that. Although we have more

important things to plan at the moment. Like when we'll see each other again. We don't even have each other's phone numbers or email addresses."

"This is true."

"Are you having second thoughts?" she asked. "What if you get home and change your mind, realizing all of this was crazy?"

"I won't change my mind. And you?"

"I won't change my mind, either. I guess I'm just nervous."

"This is normal. We're making some big changes in our lives." He smiled. "But there's no reason for this to be stressful. I think I know a way to make this transition more casual."

"How?"

"Let's go on a date."

"What do you mean?"

He pointed to the middle of the Golden Gate Bridge. "How about if we meet out there in the middle of the bridge? We'll make it a date. That will be the next time we talk to or see each other."

Sydney followed the direction of his hand to the Golden Gate Bridge. "When?"

He shrugged. "When do you think you can get your life organized where you would be comfortable seeing me and proceeding forward?"

She looked deep in thought. "Without stress?" He nodded. She let out a nervous laugh. "A month."

"No problem. Why don't we do this? You and I will

meet exactly one month from today." He checked his watch. "At ten in the morning."

"One month from today?"

"Yes. In the middle of the Golden Gate Bridge."

She thought about it for a moment and then looked back out at the Golden Gate Bridge. "I like that idea. Funny . . . I suddenly feel a little less pressure."

He smiled. "Good."

"But then what?"

"What do you mean?"

"Where do we go from there? I see you in the middle of the Golden Gate Bridge and—"

"I think the first thing would be a kiss. Or a few . . ."

"Will you answer me seriously?"

"I was being serious. But after the kisses, why don't we just find out when we see each other? If we have the faith, if we believe we were made for each other, if we are ready . . . everything will work out the way it's supposed to. Nothing will stand in our way. And honestly, there's no need to rush this. Let's enjoy the anticipation."

She nodded. "So. What are you saying? No emails or phone numbers?"

He shook his head. "None."

"That's kind of scary."

"Yes, I agree. And exciting . . ." He thought about it for a moment. "But it would be nice to know what city you live in."

"Mountain View. And you?"

"Palo Alto. Not that far from you at all."

She nodded. "What if one of us doesn't show?"

"I'll be there."

"I'll be there, too. But what if one of us doesn't show?" She poked him in the chest. "Answer the question."

"You're so feisty." They shared a nervous laugh together. "If one of us doesn't show . . . then we need to respect that. We'll go on with our lives, wishing nothing but the best for the other person. No hard feelings."

She thought about it a little longer. "One month from today at ten in the morning."

"Yes."

"Okay. It's a date."

CHAPTER FOURTEEN

"I'm in the mood to get drunk," blurted out Sydney. "Driver, can you find the nearest bar?"

"No!" yelled Gina, causing the driver to slow the car down. "Sorry, please take us home as planned." Gina cocked her head to the side and stared at Sydney. "You're finally starting to crack up. I wondered when this would happen. It's not even lunchtime yet and you already want to hit the bottle."

Sydney stared out the shuttle van window as it cruised down Highway 101. "I think I have to pee."

Gina laughed and placed her hand on Sydney's knee. "No, you don't. Everything will be okay. Take a deep breath."

Sydney took a deep breath and let it out slowly. "Okay, no pee, but maybe I should cry. I'd still be keeping it in the liquid family."

"That's disgusting. I've never heard you talk like this! I thought you were sure about Oscar?"

"I am. I am. How could I not be? It's just . . . I'm not looking forward to delivering the news to Elliot. Plus, we'll have to send out Forget-About-The-Date cards."

"Better than getting married to the wrong person."

Sydney nodded. "True."

Twenty minutes later, the driver took the Moffett Boulevard exit toward downtown Mountain View. After a few rights and a left, he pulled the van directly in front of Sydney's house. Just the sight of Elliot's white BMW in the driveway sent her heart rate up.

"Sure you don't want a drink? Driver, does this van have a mini-bar?"

The driver looked at her in the rearview mirror and shook his head.

Gina hugged her. "You'll be fine."

Sydney sighed. "Okay. Showtime."

"Don't procrastinate. Just get it done. Then pack up some things and come over. I'll have a gin fizz waiting for you as soon as you walk in the door. I promise."

"Thanks. I love you."

"I love you, too."

Sydney slid out of the van and paused for a moment, sticking her head back in. "If you love me so much, maybe you could do the breaking up for me . . ."

"Go!"

"Right. Here I go."

The driver pulled Sydney's suitcase from the back of

the van and she tipped him ten dollars. Gina waved and blew a kiss to Sydney.

Sydney forced a smile and turned toward the front door, taking a deep breath. "Let's do this."

She opened the door and lugged the suitcase inside. The house was quiet. She rolled her suitcase down the hallway to the bedroom. That's when she heard the shower running. She took a few steps toward the bathroom and peeked her head in. "I'm home!"

Why did she say it like that? It almost sounded like she was happy to be home.

"Welcome back!" he said, opening the shower door and sticking his head out. "How was the trip?"

"Great."

She sucked at lying.

He analyzed her for a moment and then closed the shower door. "I'll be right out."

For him "be right out" meant at least fifteen minutes so Sydney went to the kitchen and made some chamomile tea. Maybe it would help her calm down a little. She sipped on the tea and waited for him.

Fifteen minutes later, Elliot entered the kitchen and held out his arms. "I missed you."

She stood and hugged him back. If she said she had missed him too, she'd be lying. If she said nothing he'd wonder what was wrong. She was screwed. It was best to reply with a question.

"How do you have time to miss me when you're so busy working?"

He kissed her on the forehead. "Even on the craziest, most stressful days I think of you and miss you. Anyway, I'm glad you caught me. I'm only in town tonight. I fly back out in the morning to Dallas for four days." He lifted her chin. "Are you okay? You don't look like someone who just came home from an amazing cruise. Not what you expected?"

"Definitely not. Let's sit."

Elliot sat next to her, now a concerned look on his face. "Something happened . . ."

She nodded and hesitated. Then she said it. "I'm sorry. I can't marry you."

Elliot stared at her for a moment. He crossed his arms and his lower lip started to quiver.

Was he going to cry? It looked like it. His eyes began to fill. It didn't make sense. She was the crier, not him! This was just going to make it worse!

He sniffed. "What did I do wrong?"

Sydney let out a deep breath. "Nothing. I just realized we want different things. You have your career, which is wonderful. You love it. But you travel so much and the bottom line is I'd like a man who's around."

And I want more passion.

Within a few seconds Elliot was bawling like a baby.

This was certainly unexpected.

As vice president of sales, Elliot handled stress better than anyone. He played football in college and once played an entire game with a broken foot. He had a tattoo on his right bicep that said *This gun is loaded*. She had never seen him cry before.

Ever.

Sydney jumped up to grab some tissue, handing it to him.

He blew his nose and handed the tissue back to her. "Why does this always happen to me?"

The question caught Sydney by surprise. "You were engaged to someone before me?"

Elliot snapped his fingers and pointed to the box of tissue. She jumped up again, but this time grabbed the entire box and handed it to him.

He pulled some tissues out, wiped his nose, and nodded. "I was engaged in college for a week. Mary Sue was her name. We met in some country bar when the team traveled to Fresno to play the Bulldogs. When she found out I wasn't drafted by a professional team she broke up with me. I cried all night, which is probably what I'll be doing after you leave."

She rubbed him on the arm just below his tattoo. "I'm sorry."

Tears began to flow again for him, but there was nothing she could do. She said what she had to say. She was glad it was a peaceful breakup. No yelling. No name-calling. He'd be okay. Elliot would meet someone perfect for him when the time was right.

He sniffled and inspected the empty box. "Do we have any more tissue?"

Oscar paced back and forth in his bedroom. He had unpacked and stuck the suitcase up on the rafters in the garage. Now he just had to play the waiting game. Alexa had texted and said she'd be home in a few minutes. She had gone to the grocery store to pick up some things so she could make Oscar's favorite meal this evening. She called it his *Welcome home I love you* meal.

That didn't make it any easier. And she certainly wouldn't be in the cooking mood after he broke up with her. Too bad. Her rigatoni was the best, but delaying the breakup just to have one last plate would be wrong.

Oscar was excited about the next chapter in his life. One month seemed like a long time to wait to see Sydney, but he'd have waited longer, even six months or a year. Yes, it would have been torture at times, but he had to look at the big picture.

The future.

And it involved wonderful Sydney. He also had to figure out the best time to quit his job. Money wasn't an issue, so he didn't have to worry about that, but he didn't want to leave the company without helping them with a backup plan. The main thing was he was back. Back with his passion for photography and ready to travel the world again shooting.

He'd also have to start thinking about his living situation. Hopefully, Alexa would move out right away, but he wondered if Sydney would consider moving in. Or maybe he'd sell the house and start fresh with her. It didn't matter. What mattered was he and Sydney were together.

"Honey, I'm home!" Alexa yelled from the other room. "Help me with the bags!"

"Coming!" Oscar headed down the hallway and into the garage. He made his way to the back of the car and was received with a kiss on the cheek, of course.

Alexa smiled. "I've got so much to tell you about the wedding. I've made some changes. You'll love it." She disappeared inside the house with the two reusable shopping bags before he could answer.

He grabbed the last two bags from the back seat of the car and closed the door, heading inside to the kitchen.

As he entered the kitchen she swung around, her eyes wide and bright. "Did you think of me while you were on the cruise?"

"Of course." Occasionally.

"Okay, I want to hear about the cruise and I'm glad you didn't get swallowed by a whale or crushed by an iceberg but I need to tell you something." Alexa screamed. "I hired a band!"

"A band? What happened to the DJ?"

"It's the best of both worlds! Come on, I love the variety of music a DJ has and of course the original versions of the songs, but there's something about live music. You know?"

He nodded, wondering why he even was having this conversation. He needed to break up with her right now.

She frowned and approached Oscar. "You don't like

the idea? I did it for you! I did a lot of research and they're the only band in the United States that plays current hits plus the classics in both English and Spanish."

"Alexa . . ."

"We'll have to fly them in from Miami and put them up in a hotel for a few nights, but no big deal. Also, I want to release a thousand doves into the sky after we say I do and kiss! Wouldn't that be amazing?"

"Alexa, please."

She moved closer and tried to kiss him and he stepped back. She stared at him for a few moments. "What's going on?"

This was it. He had to do it now.

He shrugged. "We need to talk."

"Okay . . . this doesn't sound good."

"There's no easy way to say this . . . I can't marry you."

She took a step back and then grabbed the edge of the kitchen counter. "You're not serious."

"I am. I'm sorry."

"You've got cold feet. Everybody gets them. Don't worry, you'll feel better after a hot shower and a beer." She let out a nervous laugh and grabbed a binder from the counter. "Quit being silly and help me pick out some favors from this catalogue." She flipped through the pages. "We should get our guests these darling sterling silver picture frames and also—"

"It's not cold feet," he continued. "I tried to tell you before I left, but you wouldn't let me."

She closed the binder and stared at him for a few seconds. "This is *not* funny."

"I know it's not."

"You're seriously telling me the wedding is off?"

"Yes."

"And it's not cold feet."

"No."

She nodded and thought about it for a few moments. Then she picked up the binder and slammed it into his forehead. "How could you do this?" She pushed him back into the stove. Good thing she hadn't started cooking yet. She came after him again with the binder and he ran around to the other side of the kitchen table. She screamed and pointed at him. "How dare you! What about my wedding?"

"Your wedding? It was supposed to be *our* wedding."

She pulled the package of pasta out of the shopping bag and hurled it at him. He ducked and it flew right by, smacking into the wall and dropping to the floor.

"Alexa, please. You need to—"

"Stop! I don't even want to hear another word from you. Daddy will be pissed when he hears about this. So much planning and money down the drain."

"Why would he be mad? I was the one paying for the wedding."

"You just don't get it!"

She was right. He didn't.

She stormed out of the kitchen and headed to the

bedroom. Oscar touched his forehead. He'd have a bump, but at least there was no major damage.

He heard Alexa down the hallway banging around. Better to stay in the kitchen and out of harm's way. She had looked a little bit on edge there. A few minutes later, she returned to the kitchen with her gym bag over her shoulder.

"I obviously can't stay here tonight. I'll be back tomorrow to get the rest of my things, so make sure you aren't here during the day."

"Alexa, I—"

She held up her hand to stop him from saying another word and walked out.

Oscar took a deep breath and let it out. "Could have been a lot worse . . ."

CHAPTER FIFTEEN

One month later . . .

Sydney slid a hanger to the left. Then another. And another. Then she slid a hanger to the right. Then another. And another.

A few seconds later, she screamed. "Please help me! I don't know what to wear!"

Gina laughed and entered the walk-in closet. "You're a mess. And since when do you ever worry about what to wear? Be yourself. Jeans and a blouse."

Sydney sighed. "You're right, you're right." She took a blouse from one of the hangers and pulled her jeans from the shelf. "Why am I so nervous?"

"Because you're going to meet the most gorgeous and intelligent man in the world and begin the next amazing chapter of your life. I would be hyperventilating right now, so you're actually doing quite well."

Sydney laughed. "You don't get nervous."

"Yeah, well, you don't either usually, but this is different. I'm so happy for you!"

"I'm happy for me, too, but I don't feel so great."

"Let's be honest, most of your anxiety comes from your job."

"True."

Work had been more stressful than normal and she was ready to quit. Her boss had put too much on her plate and it wasn't fair. He'd even called her three times this morning even though she had taken a personal day off.

She hoped Oscar was serious about working together as a team and traveling the world because she was ready. She was ready to live her passion and get the stress out of her life before it killed her. Ready to be together with an amazing Spanish man.

She slipped on her jeans and the red blouse. "I want to scream again."

"Let it out, sista!"

She screamed and they both laughed and hugged.

Gina rubbed Sydney's arm. "Do you know what the plan is today?"

"I have no idea. He just said we would meet in the middle of the bridge. Other than that—no clue."

"As long as it involves kissing it doesn't really matter."

"I agree."

Gina had been wonderful letting Sydney stay with her

over the last month and doing so much to make her feel right at home. Sydney had to figure out where she would live, but didn't want to make a decision until she saw Oscar. She was excited and nervous, but she felt positive.

She was doing the right thing.

Forty minutes later, Sydney drove up 19th Avenue in her silver Honda Accord. The phone rang and she checked the caller ID. Her boss.

"I'm not answering!"

She threw the phone back on the passenger seat and let it go to voicemail. The guy was unbelievable. She took a deep breath and tried to forget about him.

The closer she got to the Golden Gate Bridge, the more her heart banged in her chest. She couldn't ever recall a time when she had been so nervous. Maybe back when she was a sophomore in high school and had gotten her first kiss from Zachary, the boy who sat across from her in her English class. No. She was more nervous now.

The phone rang again and she wanted to scream. She grabbed it from the passenger seat and looked at the caller ID again. Of course, her boss.

Sydney wanted to throw the phone out the window. Instead, she turned it off. As she passed San Francisco City College she felt a sharp pain in her temple. She rubbed the side of her head and the pain returned again. Sharper. Longer. Then both of her eyes twitched.

"What's going on?"

Keeping one hand on the steering wheel, she used the other hand to rub her eyes.

More pain.

More twitching.

Then everything went blank.

It was like someone had blindfolded her with a white sheet. Light was getting through but nothing else. She couldn't see a thing.

Panic set in as she gripped the steering wheel hard and took her foot off of the accelerator. She could hear the cars passing on her left and the person behind her began honking their horn. She kept the steering wheel straight and gently applied the brakes. She didn't want to be rear-ended and she didn't want to crash into anyone, either. The car came to a complete stop and she stuck it in park.

Her breathing was even heavier than before. Her heart pounded. She didn't know what to do.

"This isn't good. Not good at all."

It was like one of those nightmares that made your body jump in bed, waking you up. But she wasn't asleep. This was real. She couldn't see a thing. She could hear cars continue to pass on the left. At least the person behind her stopped honking.

She needed to get out of the car. Right now!

Sydney opened her door and slid out, careful to keep her body as close to her car as possible. Her hands ran along the roofline of her Accord as she slid sideways toward the back of the car. All she hoped for at the moment was to get out of the way of the cars and get onto the sidewalk. Then she would figure out a way to get to the bridge to meet Oscar.

"What the hell are you doing?" yelled a male voice from a car that passed by. "Get the hell out of the street, you drunk!"

Her heart pounded in her chest. "Help me!"

The man didn't answer.

Another honk from the car after that. And another honk. The sound of the passing cars got louder, like they were on top of her. She wanted to curl up into a ball and cry.

"Miss!" She heard footsteps running in her direction from behind her car. Someone gripped her arm and led her to the sidewalk. "Easy there . . . Step up here."

Sydney's eyes burned. "Oscar is waiting for me."

"Pardon me?"

Sydney felt tears travel down her face. "Please help me. I need to get to the Golden Gate—"

It was a beautiful day and Oscar was on top of the world. Soon he would be in the middle of the Golden Gate Bridge kissing the beautiful, feisty woman who had been on his mind non-stop over the last month. He pulled over and got out of the car after he spotted a bakery off of 19th Avenue. He hadn't planned on stopping but he couldn't pass up the opportunity.

Five minutes later, he was back in the car and driving up 19th Avenue toward the bridge. He glanced over at the bag from the bakery on his passenger seat and smiled. He'd had the last-minute idea of buying eclairs and he considered himself lucky that this particular bakery had them.

"Uh oh . . ."

Something was happening up ahead on the road, most likely an accident, and the right lane was blocked completely. He switched lanes and inched his way closer and closer to the emergency vehicles. There was a police car, a tow truck, a fire truck, and an ambulance. The paramedics were helping someone on the ground as a Honda Accord was being towed away.

It was such a shame to see things like that and he hoped the person was okay. Life was so unpredictable. He shook his head and thought about the contrast. That person wasn't having a good day, while Oscar was in heaven, on the way to meet the woman of his dreams.

Oscar entered the lot at the foot of the bridge and found a parking spot right in front of the souvenir shop. He glanced at the clock on the dashboard. He had fifteen minutes to get to the middle of the bridge and didn't want to be late. He grabbed the bag of eclairs, jumped out of the car, and closed the door. He began to walk and stopped, looking back at his car.

The weather in San Francisco was unpredictable and he thought about taking a jacket. He checked the sky— nothing but blue for what seemed miles. The temperature was absolutely perfect, too. Almost everyone around him was dressed in summer clothes, dresses, shorts, t-shirts.

He'd probably be okay. He decided against the jacket and headed toward the bridge.

As he walked along the rail he glanced out at the San Francisco Bay. It was just a month ago he was on the cruise ship passing right underneath it. So much had happened since then. After breaking up with Alexa, he had given notice at his company and had promised he would help them find a replacement. He didn't want to leave them hanging, so he had also agreed to be available as a consultant. He sold all the company shares and would soon begin working on a website and business plan for Oscar and Sydney's new adventure. They would make a great team, traveling the world together.

A few minutes later, he approached the middle of the bridge and looked around. It was a busy place since most tourists stopped there to take pictures of the bay and downtown San Francisco. She hadn't arrived yet. He checked his watch. Exactly ten o'clock. It wouldn't be a surprise if she was running late. That emergency scene he had passed back on 19th Avenue could have created a bit of a traffic jam.

He looked out at the bay and wondered what she would be wearing. He flashed back to the day in Victoria when they went to visit Isabella. They were wearing the same thing. He smiled. It would be funny if they were matching again today.

Over the next two hours at least thirty people had asked Oscar if he wouldn't mind taking their pictures. He didn't have a problem with it since he had nothing to do as he waited for Sydney. He checked his watch again and sighed. Was he clear on the time? He was pretty sure he was.

He started to worry. What if she didn't show up? He'd be devastated, but he hadn't thought of that possibility because she had sounded certain she'd be there. Maybe they'd messed up the time. No way would he leave now. He would wait this out as long as he could.

Five hours after their agreed meeting time Oscar's back was getting sore from standing in the same place without moving so much. And there was a chill in the air. He looked up and noticed the marine layer drifting overhead. Not good. The temperature had dropped at least ten degrees in the last half hour and he didn't have a jacket. Plus, he was getting hungry. No, he was past that. He was starving. He lifted the bag of eclairs and opened it, sticking his nose inside for a little sniff. What a wonderful smell.

He pulled one of the eclairs out and took a bite, chewing it slowly and savoring the flavor, so he didn't end up eating it all. He took a few more bites and then decided to eat the whole thing. He pulled a napkin from the bag to wipe his mouth and felt better, even though the temperature had dropped again.

Another fifteen minutes later, the fog was so thick he couldn't see anything around the bay. Not Alcatraz. Not Ghirardelli Square. Not Downtown San Francisco. He dropped his gaze to the water directly below the bridge and could barely see that! The fog and San Francisco went hand-in-hand but today it seemed like they were taking their relationship to the extreme.

Oscar was now shivering.

He huddled down on the lip of the cement below the rail and wrapped his arms around his legs. He wasn't sure how much longer he would wait.

Did she change her mind? Were her feelings not as strong as his? He was pretty sure they were. Where was she?

If she didn't show up he was pretty confident he could track her down online. But he wouldn't. They had an agreement. He remembered his words like he had said them yesterday.

If one of us doesn't show, then we need to respect that. We will go on with our lives, wishing nothing but the best for the other person. No hard feelings.

He pulled the other eclair out of the bag and ate it as he continued to shiver. His hands were frozen and his nose was running. He finished the second eclair and sat there silently. Motionless. The numbness in his body wasn't caused by the cold temperature and the fog. It was brought on by the fact she wasn't coming. His throat tightened and his breathing slowed. He had waited long enough.

Six hours.

She's not coming.

Obviously, she didn't love him like he had thought. He stood and took a deep breath. He fought back tears. Then he walked back to his car and drove home.

CHAPTER SIXTEEN

Sydney sat up in her hospital bed, still unable to see. The last two days had been frustrating since the doctors weren't any closer to finding out what exactly was wrong with her. The good news was they were confident it wasn't anything life threatening. How they were able to determine that without knowing her illness was beyond her, but she wanted to believe them.

It had been horrifying for her to lose her sight while driving, but she was grateful she didn't crash and hurt someone. She wished she knew who had helped her to the curb that day and called 911 for help. She wanted to thank him but she never found out his name since she had fainted in his arms. Next thing she knew she was in the back of an ambulance on the way to the hospital.

Nothing was more painful to her than knowing Oscar had waited for her on the Golden Gate Bridge. Her heart ached whenever she thought about it, which was just about all the time. How long had he waited? It didn't matter now. They had a deal. If one of them didn't show up, they were supposed to go on with their lives and wish the other one well. Besides, she didn't want his pity.

She sniffed. No. She refused to cry. What she needed was to rid the negative thoughts out of her head because they wouldn't do her any good. She had to remain strong and think positively that everything would turn out fine. She could beat this. Whatever it was.

She felt the touch of a hand on top of hers and she jumped.

"Sorry, I shouldn't sneak up on you like that."

Gina was still there—not a surprise. She was the best friend a person could have. She had been there non-stop since Sydney arrived, only going home yesterday for an hour to shower. She had slept on the chair next to her hospital bed the last two nights.

Sydney placed her hand on top of Gina's. "No, no. I heard you approaching and should have expected it. At least I'm getting better."

The first time Gina touched her yesterday she had jumped so high she had punched her best friend in the chin. Gina had said she was okay, but Sydney wished she could see for herself.

"Yeah, you almost knocked me out the first time."

They shared a laugh together and Sydney grabbed Gina's hand and squeezed it.

"You keep that sense of humor," said Doctor Kranz, his voice getting closer. "They weren't kidding when they said laughter is the best medicine." She could hear some papers rustling. "I got the results back from the latest round of tests and unfortunately we didn't learn anything new."

"That is so not what I wanted to hear."

"I understand. We thought there was a possibility you had something called fleeting blindness," he continued. "The temporary blindness can result from a stroke, Parkinson's disease, and lupus. We have already ruled out all of them but it could even come from a migraine. You mentioned you had a couple of sharp pains before you lost your sight."

"Yes, but it wasn't a migraine. I'm sure of it. I've had migraines in the past and the pain was unbearable. What I had in the car were like short little bursts of pain. Like someone sticking me with a needle. Then it disappeared."

"Okay, okay. Well, the only thing we can do right now is run a couple more tests, although honestly we've done almost all of them. Dr. Fico suggested it could be neurological and we're trying to get in touch with a specialist. We'll keep you updated, of course."

She frowned as Dr. Kranz walked away. "Neurological? Great, I'm psychotic."

Gina laughed. "Hey, didn't you say Isabella's husband worked in neurology?"

Sydney nodded. "He's an expert. He even led some research teams for an institute in London. But he's in Victoria, so that won't do us much good."

"I still think you should have them get in touch. What if they talk on the phone or do a video consultation?"

Not a bad idea, but if Ben knew about her condition, Isabella would know. That meant Oscar would find out. Sydney didn't want that to happen. "Forget about it. I don't want Oscar to know what happened to me."

"So, you'd give up being cured because of the possibility of being embarrassed?"

"It's not a possibility—it's a certainty. Bring your face closer to me."

"Are you going to slap me?"

"Of course not. Bring it closer."

A few seconds later, she could hear Gina's breathing and she reached out to touch her face. She ran her fingers along Gina's cheek, under her chin and over to her other cheek. Then she touched her mouth.

"Just as I suspected," said Sydney. "You've got a smug look on your face."

"Ha! You know me so well. But you need to forget about what Oscar thinks. If there is a chance Ben can help you, you need to take it."

"I'm serious, Gina. I can't face Oscar this way. Look at me. I'm helpless."

Her eyes burned.

Gina squeezed her hand. "Don't you cry. Listen to me. What if I can get Dr. Ben to promise not to say anything to Oscar?"

"You would need more than that. You would need Isabella to promise the same thing, but good luck with that one. They're two of the closest siblings I've ever seen."

"So if I get them both to promise, you're okay with it then?"

Sydney thought about it for a few seconds. "Of course."

Gina kissed her on the cheek. "Good girl. What's his last name?"

"Nicholls. Dr. Benjamin Nicholls in Victoria, BC."

The next day Ben kissed Sydney on both cheeks. "How's the patient?"

"I could go for some coffee."

Ben chuckled. "I'm sure Dr. Kranz told you to avoid caffeine."

"That he did, unfortunately."

It had touched her heart so deeply when she found yesterday that Ben would arrive today, but she also felt bad he'd dropped everything to fly there. She'd assumed if there was a possibility Ben could help he would have talked with Dr. Kranz on the phone or would have done a video consultation, not get on a plane and fly a thousand miles. Something told her everything would be fine now that Ben was involved.

"I have something special for you. Hold out your hand, but be careful. It's fragile."

Sydney held out her hand and he placed something in it. Whatever it was had a plastic wrapper on it. She felt it gently but couldn't figure out what it was. "I give up."

"It's a fortune cookie."

"Ahh! Real food!" She laughed and tore the plastic off it and then broke the fortune cookie in half. She pulled out the fortune and frowned. "Oh . . . I guess you'll have to read it." She held out the fortune for him to take and she crunched a bite of the cookie.

Ben cleared his throat and read the fortune. "You will prepare scones for any doctor who visits from out of the area."

Sydney almost choked on her cookie and laughed. "You're obsessed with scones! If Isabella was here she'd tell you to prepare them yourself."

"That's for sure," said Isabella.

Sydney stopped chewing. "Isabella . . ."

Oscar's sweet sister was there. She had traveled all the way from Victoria with Ben. What an amazing gesture of kindness and friendship. She felt tears coming on.

"No, no," said Gina. "No crying!"

Sydney wiped her eyes and held out her arms. "Fine, but I have to hug Isabella. Thank you so much for coming —it means so much to me."

"My pleasure." Isabella kissed Sydney on both cheeks and then hugged her. "So good to see you."

"You, too." Sydney's hand flew over her mouth.

"What is it?" asked Ben.

"Nothing. It's just . . . I realized what I had said. I said it was good to see Isabella. Obviously I can't . . ."

"This is completely normal. We have so many habits ingrained in us we can practically do them while we're sleeping. So, let me tell you what I've come up with so far. Dr. Kranz sent me all of your files and test results and I was able to go over them a couple of times. Right now I'm almost convinced I know what's causing your blindness."

"That's amazing. What is it?"

"A conversion disorder."

"Okay . . . What's that and how did I get it?"

"Stress is the underlying cause. There's only so much a body can handle before it reaches a certain breaking point. That's when the mental stress converts into something physical."

"Amazing," said Gina.

"It is," said Ben. "Has there been anything in your life recently that has been stressing you out, making you nervous?"

"Well, my job is stressful, for one. I want to kill my boss —he's driving me crazy. Wait. Is that what happened? Did he drive me nuts?"

Ben chuckled. "I doubt it, but stress is common in the workplace. Conversion disorder can come from severe cases of work stress or something more traumatic on a personal level. For example, the loss of a parent or spouse."

Her parents were still alive, happy and living in North Carolina. On top of the stressful job, she had broken up with Elliot. Plus she had had to move. Then there was the anxiety of meeting Oscar on the bridge.

"What?" asked Gina. "Did you think of something? Your mouth is hanging open."

"Uh . . ." She closed her mouth and thought about it.

"Okay, I'll tell you in the interest of medicine and because I'd like to get better. I had been anxious thinking of meeting Oscar." She gasped. "No! You're saying that Oscar freaked me out?"

Ben laughed. "I'm not sure. It could be a combination of things—the stress from the job and the anxiety of meeting Oscar. A lot of studies have been done on it that date back to Sigmund Freud, and conversion disorder can vary quite a bit from what I've read and seen. So, here's the deal. I'd like to do one more test. An EEG scan can help rule out a neurological cause. It's a painless procedure that will detect electrical activity in your brain."

"And if I have it? Is it permanent?"

"Not always. Symptoms can be relatively brief, with the average duration around two weeks."

"I can live with that."

"Well . . . that's the average, though. Keep in mind that there are some cases where it can last a couple months or years. In some cases it can be permanent."

"Wow . . ."

"I prefer not to speculate. I'll get you set up for the test and we can take it from there. Let me know if you notice any changes at all, even small ones. A sense of more light entering, eye twitching, eyelid tics, spasms, pain, anything. Usually the body sends you a message when things are getting better, so try to be alert to those."

"Thank you so much. You haven't mentioned anything to Oscar, have you?"

"We gave Gina our word," said Isabella, squeezing

Sydney's shoulder. "But I'll be honest with you—I don't think this is something you should keep from him. He cares about you."

"I don't want him to see me until this goes away. I can't."

"Fine. I'll be back tomorrow to try to convince you again."

Sydney laughed. "Good luck."

It was good to laugh, considering what had happened. She couldn't imagine not being able to see for two years. And worst case scenario, permanently. What would she do? How would she be able to function on a daily basis? She'd seen blind people around town occasionally and had always wondered what their lives were like. Now she was one of them. She wouldn't be able to team up with Oscar to travel the world and document it. How could she write about something she couldn't even see?

She couldn't.

But she wondered what Oscar was doing at that moment. Was he heartbroken? Was he already trying to move on with his life? Maybe once Ben finished working on her blindness, he could figure out how to mend her broken heart.

But she knew he didn't have a cure for that.

CHAPTER SEVENTEEN

Sydney's hands were sweaty. "I'm nervous."

Gina squeezed her arm. "Don't worry, I'll be watching you."

"And why are we doing this?"

Gina laughed. "You need to get out of the house and do things like a normal person."

She didn't feel like a normal person, but at least she'd come to terms with her vision. She would just have to wait it out and eventually her sight would return.

"Okay," said Gina. "Let's go. I'll show you what it's like to have fun again." Gina took her hand and led Sydney to the garage. "I'll help you into the car."

Sydney shook her hand free from Gina's. "Let me do this."

"Now you're talking!"

Sydney followed the hood of the car with her hand to

the passenger side and found the door handle, opening it. She slid into the car carefully and clicked her seatbelt in place.

She was nervous and excited. Gina wanted to surprise her by taking her to a concert, but she wouldn't say who they were going to see.

Gina pulled out of the garage and Sydney felt the sun hit her chest and legs. She could sense the brightness with her eyes, even though she couldn't see a thing. She opened her purse and pulled out her sunglasses, putting them on. She'd feel a little less self-conscious in public with her eyes covered.

Sydney remained silent as Gina drove, trying to see if she could figure out what street they were on by the turns Gina had taken since they had left the house.

"Did you just pull onto Highway 101?"

"Yes. Quit trying to figure out the surprise."

"North, right?"

"Yes. Knock it off. Maybe this will distract you."

The sound of music filled the car and Sydney laughed. "That won't work! If you take an exit in the next two minutes I know where we're going."

Gina sighed. "That's not fair!"

Sydney heard the turn signal and felt the car go into the right lane. "I know! I know!"

"Don't say it."

"We're going to see Michael Bublé at the Shoreline Amphitheater in Mountain View." Gina didn't answer and then the radio went silent. "Gina?"

"Yes . . ."

"Am I right?"

"Yes, but I wanted it to be a surprise!"

"It *is* a surprise. I had to find out sometime, right?"

"Yeah."

Sydney reached over and patted Gina on her leg. "Thank you."

Gina was the best friend ever, always thinking of others. Sydney was grateful to have her in her life and was looking forward to spending some time with her outside.

After Gina parked, Sydney slowly opened her door and moved to the front of the car, using her hand as the guide. She waited there for Gina. A few seconds later, Gina grabbed her hand and they walked side-by-side toward the entrance.

Most of the voices she heard around them as they walked were female, which wasn't a surprise. They passed through the security and ticket gate and headed to the lawn area of the amphitheater where the majority of the people would be seated. Sydney had been there before, having seen various artists over the years. The only difference this time was she would only be able to listen. Not a bad thing at all when it came to music.

After the opening artist, there was a break and she asked Gina to take her to the bathroom. They returned and sat and waited for Michael Bublé to hit the stage. It wasn't long before the high-pitched screams filled the amphitheater. He was obviously ready to entertain. He played all of his original hits and, of course, all the big band classics that he remade. Gina and Sydney sang along to every song and even got up and danced a couple of times.

Then Michael started singing "I've Got You Under My Skin."

Sydney froze. "Oh, no . . ."

"What?" asked Gina

"This song . . ."

"I know! I love it, too."

"No. This is the one that Oscar and I—"

"Oh. The one in the ballroom in Victoria?"

"Yeah . . . You know what? I think I want to stretch. How about another drink?"

Gina helped her up. "Sounds good."

They walked toward the concessions area and waited in line.

Sydney squeezed Gina's hand. "Sorry."

"Don't be. This is a lot for you to take in for your first time out. And it's not a surprise you find things that make you think of Oscar. But I'll do my best to—"

Gina was silent. Did she lose her train of thought? Sydney wiggled her hand. "You'll do your best to what?"

"Uh . . ."

"Hello, Sydney," said the male voice that sounded exactly like Oscar.

Sydney's heart started doing the normal thumping when she was in his presence. What was Oscar doing at a Michael Bublé concert? It didn't matter. She needed to play it cool. Isabella and Ben had sworn they hadn't said anything to him about her being blind, so she needed to act natural and get rid of him.

The most Sydney could get out was one word. "Hello."

Then there was silence between them. Sydney could hear people around her but she had no idea what was going on with Oscar. His facial expression. His body language. Nothing. She reached over and pinched Gina.

"You're a big Bublé fan?" asked Gina, finally coming to the rescue. "Or someone you came with?"

"I came by myself," answered Oscar. "And yes, I think he's an amazing singer, but truthfully I wouldn't have come if he hadn't invited me."

"Michael Bublé invited you to his concert?"

"Yes, but it's not what you think. He's more friends with my sister Isabella than me."

"Really? How did that happen?"

Great. Were they going to have a conversation while Sydney uncomfortably kept her mouth shut?

Why not order some tea? Break out the scones! I'll just stand here and pretend I'm not blind.

"Michael is from Burnaby, British Columbia," said Oscar. "It's not that far from Victoria where Isabella lives. They worked together on some nonprofit event years ago and hit it off."

"What a coincidence."

"Yes."

If either of them mentioned serendipity, Sydney was going to start swinging until she connected with someone.

"That is so cool." Gina tapped Sydney on the arm. "Isn't it Sydney?"

Sydney forced a smile, but didn't answer.

More silence. Normally, Sydney enjoyed the smell of nachos, but right now they were making her nauseated. Or maybe it was just the thought of Oscar figuring out what was going on. Her heart ached again. She longed to see his face. She wanted another dance. Another kiss. But she couldn't bring herself to do it. She didn't know if what she had was permanent or temporary. If it was permanent, she'd be a hindrance to his life. She'd slow him down. She knew what it was like to do something she didn't enjoy. She felt dead inside. And she wouldn't be the cause of him feeling the same way.

Sydney's eyes burned. Good thing she had her sunglasses on—they would cover the moisture. But still, the silence killed her.

Oscar cleared his throat. "Okay. I guess I'll be going then. Goodbye, Sydney."

"Goodbye."

A few seconds later, Gina squeezed her arm. "What were you thinking? The man of your dreams was standing right in front of you."

"I just couldn't."

"What are the chances you would run into him here? And on the first day you left the house in such a long time? What happened to serendipity?"

"Don't use that word! It hurts."

"You're trying to fight it but you'll lose. Serendipity is alive and well in my life because of you and Oscar."

Sydney turned toward her voice. "You believe in serendipity?"

"Close your mouth before a bug flies in and you choke to death. You and Oscar were meant to be together—it's so obvious. And I'll tell you something right now, so you better listen up. If you don't do something about it, I will."

Oscar felt like crap as he entered the backstage area again. He stood off to the side of the stage as Michael Bublé sang, "Just Haven't Met You Yet." It was wonderful to see Sydney, but it was like they had never met before. She wouldn't even engage in a conversation with him. She couldn't even look in his direction. She just stood there while he talked with Gina. He liked Gina but he had wanted to talk to Sydney.

He wanted to ask Sydney why she hadn't shown up at the bridge, but they had agreed to respect the other person's decision if they didn't show up. Still, he was hoping for a sign that they still had a chance. That she still felt something for him. He had thought about inviting her backstage since he had a couple of extra passes in his pocket. It would have been wonderful to see her face after she'd met Michael and had taken pictures with him after the show. But she acted as if she didn't want to be in his presence. Like she was disgusted with him. She just ignored him. It didn't make sense at all. The way she wouldn't maintain eye contact. The way she held on so tight to Gina's arm. Something was off.

Better to not think of her. Then maybe the pain would go away.

Michael finished his set and came offstage, walking in Oscar's direction. He looked sharp in his gray suit and tie with black shoes.

He smiled and hugged Oscar. "Glad you made it. How's Isabella?"

"She's great. What about you? How's the family?"

Michael smiled. "Getting bigger. Can't complain at all. Look, I've only got one minute and then I'm going back out for an encore. We head to the airport for Las Vegas directly after so I won't be able to chat then. You got your phone on you?"

Oscar pulled his cell out of his pocket. "Of course."

"Great. Let's do a quick selfie and then email it to me. I want to stick it on my Facebook page."

"You got it." Oscar held out his phone in front of them and snapped a picture. "Got it."

Michael hugged him again. "Okay, my friend. Until next time . . ."

As Michael went back out for an encore, Oscar's cell phone vibrated in his hand. His brother-in-law, Ben. He rarely received phone calls from him. He hoped everything was all right.

He answered the call. "Just one second, Ben. I won't be

able to hear you, so let me get out of the backstage area."
Oscar headed back out to a more quiet area to talk. "Okay.
Are you there?"

"I'm here. Sounds like you're at the concert."

"I am. Is everything okay?"

He hesitated. "Honestly, we really don't know what's
going on. Isabella complained of severe stomach pains, so I
took her into emergency."

"Please tell me she's okay."

"Right now we don't know anything at all, but I
wanted to keep you in the loop. They're running some tests
on her and I'm sure we'll know soon if—"

"I'll be on the next flight."

Oscar hung up without saying another word. He ran
from the outside of the amphitheater to the parking lot and
got in his car. On the freeway he called and found a flight
leaving for Seattle. Then he could easily get a connecting
flight from there to Victoria. Realistically, he could be in
the hospital standing next to his sister, holding her hands,
in a little over four hours. He bought the one-way ticket
and hung up as he took the San Jose International Airport
exit off the freeway.

He parked in short-term parking and ran toward the
terminal. Out of breath, he got to the security line and
showed them the boarding pass on his cell phone, along
with his ID. He arrived at the gate as the agent called over
the PA system to start boarding families with any small
children.

He sat, took a deep breath and tried to relax.

His sister was everything to him and he'd be crushed if anything happened to her. He needed to be there for her. Something in Ben's voice hadn't sounded right and Oscar certainly couldn't wait around for the doctor's diagnosis. What if something happened to her? He'd almost lost her once and that was the most difficult period in his life. Only one other event brought that much pain, the day he waited for Sydney on the Golden Gate Bridge. But at least Sydney was okay. She just didn't love him, which was pretty evident by her behavior today at the concert.

He pulled the travel magazine from the seat-back pocket and flipped through the pages. He stopped on the advertisement for Alaska. He shook his head, thinking of Sydney again. He wanted to ask her why she didn't meet him on the bridge. Why she didn't care for him anymore. He needed to stop thinking about her. This was ridiculous. He tried to distract himself by flipping through more pages and froze.

"The exhibition . . ."

In all the rush of getting to the airport, Oscar had forgotten about the exhibition the next day. His photos of Alaska would be featured and he was supposed to be there in person. He would have to call the producer of the exhibition and give him the bad news when he arrived in Victoria.

Nothing he could do now. He needed to be there for his sister. That's what you do when you love someone. You stick together, through thick and thin. Nothing was more important in life than that. Not your job. Not your house. Nothing.

His mind drifted back to Sydney again. He would give her the world if he could.

Too bad she wanted nothing to do with him.

CHAPTER EIGHTEEN

Sydney was in no mood to go out again the next day, but Gina was obsessed with the idea.

Gina sighed. "I'm not taking no for an answer. I'll drag you out of the house if I have to."

Seeing Oscar yesterday really set her back and she hadn't slept well. She felt horrible not saying anything to him. She could have been more than cordial. The only words she could get out of her mouth were hello and goodbye. Eloquent. It had been amazing to be out with the sun shining on her body and the beautiful songs filling her ears. Until the point where Michael Bublé sang that one song.

Gina tugged on Sydney's arm. "Come on."

Sydney pinched her hand. "No."

"Okay . . . fine. I want you to move out."

Sydney laughed. "Nice try."

"Seriously. You obviously want to hurt my feelings and

waste my money."

"Waste your money? What are you talking about?"

"I already bought the tickets to the exhibition. The money goes to a good cause and you obviously don't care about charities."

She had no idea Gina had purchased the tickets, but she should have asked her if she wanted to go first.

Sydney let out a deep breath. "What exhibition? And what charity?"

"It's a surprise."

"Of course."

"I'm serious."

"Tell me what it is and then I'll tell you if I want to go."

"No. If you love me, you're going."

"What's love got to do with it?"

"Now you're starting to sound like Tina Turner. Come on . . ."

Sydney groaned and got up, following Gina to the garage. Sydney made her way around the car and got into the passenger side, a little faster this time. It was round two of trying to act like a normal person. On the drive, she paid attention to the turns and stops to try to guess where they were going. She was certain they were on Castro Street, and Gina had just driven over the railroad tracks near the Caltrain station.

Sydney reached over and rubbed Gina's arm as she drove. "Sorry for being so crabby. I know you mean well, but yesterday wasn't the easiest day for me."

"I know. Things will be better today. Trust me."

"I'll trust you when you tell me where we're going."

"I can't do that. And you forget about trying to figure out the turns and stops in your head. I purposely drove a different way to our destination so you'd be confused."

"That's so wrong! We're on Central Expressway, right?"

"No comment."

A few minutes later, they arrived at their destination. Gina had definitely taken some side streets because Sydney had no idea where they were. They got out of the car and Sydney listened for clues. Nothing. "Tell me."

"Shh! The show is about to start!"

"What show? We're outside in a parking lot from what I can tell."

Gina laughed and pulled her by the arm. "Come on."

As they stood in line, Sydney caught parts of conversations, but couldn't piece anything together yet. Alaska. Ice. Glaciers. But the last two words she heard from a female voice sent chills up her spine. Martin Os. That was Oscar's alias. His photographer name. Was Oscar there?

She was being set up.

This wasn't happening. Without her sunglasses, he'd be able to see her eyes and know something was wrong. She had to get out of there.

Sydney tugged on Gina's arm. "Take me home."

"Don't be silly."

"Now, Gina, I don't want to see—"

"Welcome to the Last Frontier Exhibit," said a male voice. "Remember that some of the framed images in the Grand Ballroom are being sold today and all proceeds go toward the preservation of Alaska. Unfortunately, one of the photographers, Martin Os, could not be with us today. We're sorry for the inconvenience."

A few steps inside and Sydney pulled Gina to a stop. "You did this after what happened yesterday? Why?"

"I had this planned for a while, but yesterday was serendip—"

"Don't say it." Sydney sighed. "Well, you can take me home now. Your plan failed."

Gina pulled her in a certain direction. "Why do we need to go?"

"In case you haven't noticed—" She pointed to her eyes. "I can't see."

"We're here already and—"

"What? What's going on? Is Oscar here?"

"No, but I never got to see his photos like you did in Victoria. I just want to—"

Gina stopped talking and let go of Sydney's arm.

"What happened? Gina, please. Is he here?"

"No, but you are. Oh wow, Sydney. You're on the wall. It's a picture of you and it's so beautiful."

Now Gina was starting to freak her out. "What do you mean? What picture?"

"It's a huge photo. It must be seven or eight feet wide.

You're standing on the glacier with your back to the camera. You're wearing the brown jacket with the fur-trimmed hood that I lent you. I'm so jealous. Your butt looks amazing in those jeans."

"Forget about my butt!"

"I'm serious. This is the most beautiful picture I've ever seen. Your arms are spread out wide and right above you is the most beautiful—"

"Bald eagle."

"Yes! The eagle's wings are fully expanded. How did he capture that? The timing had to be impeccable. Wow. I could stare at this picture for hours."

Sydney swallowed hard as emotions began to travel through her. She wanted to see the photo so bad it hurt. She wanted to stare at it for hours! Why did this happen to her? Why couldn't she see? Did the stress really poison her body like that? That day on the glacier was one of the many incredible days she had on the cruise with Oscar. A beautiful day with the man she loved. That's right. She loved him with all her heart. And he didn't even know.

"I'm buying that photo." There was no way anyone else would buy it. One day she would see it and appreciate it with her own two eyes. "Please tell me this is one of the photos for sale."

"It is. Hang on. Let me see how much it costs."

The price didn't matter. She was going to buy it. Even if she had to work for the rest of her life to pay it off.

"Two thousand dollars."

"Sold."

Oscar stood next to his sister's hospital bed, clutching her hand. He was happy. Grateful. Isabella would be okay. That was quite a scare he'd gotten and he'd spent the entire night there at the hospital. It was events like these that really make you sit up and pay attention. Really remind you of how precious life is and how it can be taken away from you without notice.

Isabella's episode of severe stomach pains was a case of food poisoning. They had kept her overnight for precautionary measure, but she'd be able to go back home today.

She rubbed the top of her brother's hand and smiled. "You can't fly up here every time I'm not feeling well."

"Yes, I can. It could have been appendicitis. You would have needed surgery."

She shook her head. "You're stubborn."

"I'm Spanish, just like you."

She laughed and then her face turned serious. "You don't look so well yourself. What's going on?"

He shrugged. "Sydney. I saw her yesterday at the concert."

Isabella sat up in her bed. "How did she look?"

It was Oscar's turn to analyze his sister. She was acting weird. "She looked as beautiful as ever. Of course. Is there something you'd like to tell me?"

"No, no." She played with her silver sun pendant, sliding it back and forth along the sterling silver chain. A few seconds later, she removed it from her neck and held it in her hand. Then she kissed it and handed it to Oscar. "Please give this to Sydney."

He stared at it for a few seconds then handed the chain and pendant back to her. "I won't be seeing her. And why would you want to give this to her? I don't think I've ever seen you take it off."

"Because life is short and she really liked it. I have a hundred others I can wear."

His sister didn't make any sense at all. What was she talking about? Why would Isabella give Sydney her favorite pendant? The one she had made with her own two hands?

Isabella held out the pendant and chain again. "Take it. Give it to her. Please."

"I don't even know where she is. It was a coincidence we saw each other yesterday."

Did he really say that? He knew it wasn't a coincidence. Still, Sydney obviously wanted nothing to do with him. Her not showing up at the Golden Gate Bridge had been a clear indication. And if that hadn't convinced him, her actions and lack of words at the concert yesterday spoke volumes.

"Did I just hear my own brother, Mr. Serendipity, call his encounter with Sydney a coincidence?"

He should have known she'd call him on it. "Okay. You got me there, but I was serious. I don't know where she lives."

"You're the smartest man I know. A genius. You could easily find her if you put your mind to it. But I'll take the burden from you. I have her address and will give it to you. Go and see her just to give her this gift from me. Tomorrow."

CHAPTER NINETEEN

Oscar sat in his car in front of Gina's home, staring through the passenger side window at the front door. Isabella had given him the address yesterday and had told him Sydney was staying with Gina for a while during a transition period. What transition period?

He couldn't believe he was there in front of the house after the way she had acted at the concert, but he'd use the opportunity to get some answers and closure before he moved on with his life without her.

Oscar took a deep breath and slid out of the car, heading to the front door. He stared at the doorbell for a few seconds and then pressed it. He didn't hear the ding-dong, but maybe it rang in another area of the house. He took a deep breath and then waited. No noise inside. Maybe the doorbell was broken. He pressed it again and waited. Yeah, it must be broken.

Maybe he should quit being an idiot and knock on the door. He did have knuckles.

He knocked exactly four times and waited. This time he heard movement inside the house. A few seconds later, the door swung open.

"Hi," said Gina, with a smile that told him she had no problem he was there.

"Hi." He stood there rocking back and forth on his feet. "Uh . . . is Sydney available?"

"Yes." Gina looked behind her and then turned back around. She stepped outside and closed the door. "How did you find us? Isabella?"

Oscar nodded.

"Okay. I won't say anything at all. This is between you two. Come in. She's listening to an audiobook in the backyard. She'll probably kill me but we can deal with my death later."

Oscar chuckled. "Sounds good."

He followed Gina inside through the entryway and kitchen, out to the backyard. Sydney was cuddled up on one of the patio chairs in the sun listening to the audiobook, wearing sunglasses. She looked cute in her white shorts and red T-shirt.

She obviously was enthralled with whatever she was listening to because she hadn't even noticed that Oscar stood right in front of her. Was she sleeping? Only one way to find out.

"Hello, Sydney." She jumped and almost fell out of the chair. "Sorry to startle you."

She removed the ear buds and set them on her lap. "That's okay."

He moved over to the patio chair next to her and sat. "We didn't really get a chance to talk much at the concert. How have you been?"

She shifted in her chair. "I'm hanging in there. You?"

"Not so good."

"Oh." She shifted in her chair again. "I'm sorry to hear that."

He eyed her hand. "I don't see a wedding ring on your finger. Does that mean you broke off the engagement?"

She reached over and rubbed her hand. Then she nodded.

He held up his hand. "Me, too." Sydney didn't bother looking, so he dropped it. This would be harder than he thought. "I guess that doesn't matter, does it?" She didn't answer. "Yeah. I guess not."

She shifted in her chair. "I thought we had a deal that if one of us didn't show up to the Golden Gate Bridge, the other person would just let it be and wish them well."

"True. I guess I messed that up. Kind of like how you messed it up when you said you would actually meet me there." She didn't speak. "Did you know the temperature can drop thirty degrees on the middle of the bridge when the fog and wind roll in? In a matter of minutes."

"No."

"It's true. Very common in the summer . . . Imagine a person going out there on a beautiful blue-sky day, wearing a short sleeve shirt, to meet someone special. The guy could get cold in a hurry when the fog and wind rolled in. Imagine that person out there in the cold for three hours. Or four or five. No wait, six hours. He'd probably end up sick in bed for a week or two. Well—ten days to be exact. Can you imagine someone going through that?"

"Oscar—"

"I feel sorry for the guy, don't you?"

She sighed. "Let's not do this. Please."

"You're right." He stood and pulled the pendant from his pocket and held it out to Sydney. "Isabella wanted you to have this."

She stared toward the house. "What?"

He dangled it in front of her face. "This."

She hesitated and then held out her hand. She was acting weird and he didn't know why. He placed the pendant in her palm.

She ran her fingers across the pendant, rubbing the edges, the grooves. "Carpe diem."

"Yes. This was her favorite piece of jewelry, but for some reason she wanted you to have it. She made it herself."

"I know. It's beautiful."

"Anyway, that's why I came. She wanted me to give it to you."

"Please tell her thank you. On second thought, I'll call her."

That didn't seem fair. His sister was friends with the woman who had captured his heart. Also, the woman who had broken it. Oscar's heart broke even more as he looked at the emotionless woman in front of him. He'd never misjudged a woman more in his life than her. He was finished with her. Her body language had spoken and it told him she wanted nothing to do with him.

He shrugged. "Okay, then. Guess I should be going then."

She nodded and shifted in her chair again. "Okay. Take care."

He let out a nervous chuckle. "You, too." He turned to walk away and then stopped.

As horrible as this turned out he was grateful for one thing and he had to tell her. To thank her.

He turned back around. "Before I go, I really need to say thank you."

"For what?"

"For helping me get back to my passion of photography. It was because of you. That day on the glacier helped me realize what was important in my life. I thought you were one of those important things but . . ."

She didn't answer.

"Anyway, the picture I took of you with the bald eagle, I knew it was something special. It traveled around the country with an Alaska exhibition sponsored by The Discovery Channel. I was going to give it to you. I *wanted* to give it to you. Had it framed and everything. But since you never showed up . . ."

"Yeah."

"Anyway, I donated it to them and someone bought it. A blind woman, from what they tell me. On the last day of the exhibition all the signed images were sold and the money went to the preservation of Alaska. A good cause." He was talking too much now and needed to wrap this up. "Can you believe a blind woman bought that photo of you? The funny thing is they told me she had short, strawberry-blonde hair. Just like . . . you."

Oscar blinked twice. He studied Sydney for a moment.

Sydney slid two fingers under her sunglasses and wiped her eye. Then she wiped the other eye.

"Sydney—"

"Take care, Oscar. Thank you for stopping by."

It was obvious she was trying to get rid of him now. Oscar's heart rate accelerated. He stepped forward and waved his hand in front of her face. She tilted her head to the side but didn't say anything. He waved his hand in front of her face again.

Nothing.

He swallowed hard.

He stood there deep in thought.

"Oscar, you should go now."

"I will, but . . . I need to check on something inside the house. I'll be right back."

"Check what? You really need to go."

Oscar headed inside the house and practically ran into Gina. She was crying.

He stared at her for a few seconds and tried to think clearly, piecing all of this together. "Sydney was the one who bought my photo, right?"

Gina sniffed and pointed to the first bedroom.

Oscar took a deep breath and walked toward the bedroom, pushing the door open. He stepped inside and froze. The photo of Sydney with the bald eagle. It was on the floor, leaning against the wall.

He swallowed hard again. "Sydney is blind."

Sydney waited in the backyard for Oscar to return, rocking back and forth in her chair. She thought she had pulled off the lie but was sadly mistaken. She should have known sooner or later a genius would have figured everything out.

It took every bit of her strength not to cry like a baby. Her heart raced as she rubbed her hands together. What would he do now? Scold her for lying? Pity her? That's exactly what she had wanted to avoid.

She heard the screen door slide open and close at the back of the house. His footsteps moved in her direction. He didn't say a word. She could hear him stop right in front of her. Could hear him breathing. She wanted to see his face. See how he was looking at her. Why was this happening to her? Why couldn't they be back in Victoria, dancing in the ballroom at the Empress Hotel? Kissing again.

She knew he was standing right in front of her and the silence was killing her. "Say something, Oscar. Please."

He took her hands in his and caressed them with his thumbs. "Why didn't you tell me?"

She shook her head, fighting back the tears. "I didn't want you to see me this way."

"What way? Nothing has changed." He kissed her hands and then released them. He pulled her forward on the chair, wrapped his arms around her and gave her a warm embrace. It was heaven.

Sydney felt the warmth of Oscar's hands on her cheek. He moved his fingers toward her eyes and removed her glasses. "This is why you didn't meet me on the bridge."

She nodded, a tear traveling down her cheek. "I was on my way to meet you, driving up 19th Avenue. Then everything disappeared. I couldn't see. I wanted to be there, but they towed my car and took me to the hospital."

"It's okay . . ." He wiped away her tear and kissed her on her forehead. "I saw you."

"What do you mean?"

"I mean I drove right by you on 19th Avenue when the emergency crew was with you. I saw your car, but had no idea it was you."

Sydney closed her eyes and let out a deep breath. "Ben said this could be permanent. I don't want your pity."

"Pity never crossed my mind." Oscar kissed her on her left eye, holding his lips there for a few seconds. "What about my kisses?" He kissed her right eye. "Do you want those?"

"Yes, please."

Oscar chuckled. "As you wish." He pressed his lips against hers. A few seconds later, he pulled away. "Sydney—"

"Yes."

"I love you."

Her bottom lip trembled. Tears streamed down her face. "I love you, too. I'm sorry—I should have told you."

"We're together now. That's what's important."

More tears.

She wiped her eyes and sniffled. "I must look horrible."

"If horrible is another word for breathtaking, then yes."

Oscar kissed Sydney again and her eyes began to spasm. She pulled away from him, trying to get a sense of what was happening.

"What is it?" asked Oscar.

"I'm not sure. Ben said to be aware of signals from my body. Little messages. They could be a sign of improvement. I felt a little fluttering in my eyes."

"My kisses must be therapeutic."

She laughed. "Must be. Funny, but I suddenly feel like everything is going to be okay."

"Everything's going to be more than okay. Believe it's possible and the rest will fall into place." He took the chain from Sydney's hand and fastened it around her neck. "Carpe diem."

She nodded. "Carpe diem."

"I think I'll seize this moment and give you a few more healing kisses."

EPILOGUE

One year later . . .

Oscar waited patiently on top of the Land Rover for the setting sun to drop into the perfect position, directly behind a trio of acacia trees. Fortunately, the giraffe was in no hurry to leave, still nibbling away on the leaves of one of the trees. Everything was perfect. The red, orange, and yellow of the sunset. The magnificent formation of the clouds in the sky. And the silhouette of the giraffe.

He was about to start shooting when he noticed something in his peripheral. He raised his gaze and froze. A Verreaux's eagle circled overhead.

"Look at that," Oscar whispered.

Sydney stopped typing and looked up from her laptop. "I see. You getting a déjà vu?"

"Big time. I need that eagle to fly lower and do it in the next three minutes. Otherwise we'll lose the light."

"You want me to send Big Bird a few telepathic messages?"

Oscar chuckled. "That would be greatly appreciated."

He was having the time of his life in Africa with the woman he loved. They had started in Casablanca and were working their way all the way down the continent to Cape Town. Africa, top to bottom. Oscar had gotten the idea for this trip from a wonderful book he'd read, *Safari Jema* by Teresa O'Kane. Their current location in the Serengeti was one of the highlights of the trip.

Oscar changed lenses, opting for the wide-angle panoramic fish eye.

Sydney leaned forward. "Come on, birdie, birdie."

"If you make me laugh I'll shake the camera and get blurry photos."

"Sorry. We don't want that again."

Even when they worked they had fun. It was his passion. His dream.

The eagle turned and glided, its wings fully expanded, over the acacia trees. Oscar rapid-fired a round of twenty-five photos before the eagle disappeared into the distance.

He turned to Sydney and grinned. "Got it."

Sydney leaned over and kissed Oscar on the cheek. "Not a surprise. You're the best, Mr. Martin."

"So kind of you to say so, Mrs. Martin."

He loved calling her that. Sydney was the best wife a man could ask for.

Oscar was grateful.

It was exactly a year since that day he had shown up at Gina's house and found out that Sydney was blind. That day he knew he'd never let her go. He loved her no matter what, even if she were to be blind for the rest of her life.

A few days later, she had gotten her sight back. Ben was certain that the episode had been caused by stress and had warned Sydney about recurrences if she wasn't careful. Sydney hadn't taken a chance and had quit her job. That same day she had moved in with Oscar and she hadn't had any issues since.

Three months later, they were married in the middle of the Golden Gate Bridge and had a contract to publish a travel guide with Fodor. Life was good.

Life was great!

Oscar kissed Sydney on the lips and placed his camera on the roof of the Land Rover. He slid the small ice chest closer and pulled out a bottle of water, grinning.

Sydney raised an eyebrow. "You're up to something."

She knew him so well.

Oscar shrugged and tried to play it off, grabbing a white plastic bag from the ice chest. "I have no idea what you're talking about."

Sydney glanced down at the plastic bag in Oscar's hands. She was certain she knew what was inside but tried to imagine how he had gotten it.

Oscar winked at her and peeked inside the bag. "What is this? It looks like an eclair."

"I knew it!"

He laughed and pulled the eclair out of the bag. He inhaled through his nose and smiled. "Smells like an eclair, too. Maybe I should take a bite to verify that it is indeed an eclair." He lifted the eclair to this mouth and—

"Wait!" said Sydney, scooting closer. The eclair was inches from his mouth. "Is that from the bakery this morning?"

Oscar nodded. "I went back and got it while you were in the shower."

They had spent the last two nights in Nairobi. Directly next door to the hotel was a quaint bakery that served fresh croissants, pastries, bread and the most delicious coffee she had ever enjoyed. Not a surprise since Kenya was known for having some of the best coffee in the world. What *was* a surprise was the eclair in Oscar's hand. There was no way he was going to eat it.

Sydney reached for it and Oscar pulled it away.

Oscar gave her a *tsk tsk*. "What do you think you're doing?"

"You're only teasing me. Hand it over. You won't take the first bite."

"You're right. I'm not going to take the first bite."

"Smart man."

"I'm going to take *all* the bites." He moved the eclair closer to his mouth and—

"Don't do it!" She reached for the eclair, but instead jammed it into his face.

Oscar sat there frozen. Frosting and cream covered the entire right side of his face.

Sydney tried to keep a straight face but it wasn't easy. She burst out in laughter when a chunk of the eclair slid off of his face and plopped onto his lap. "So sorry." She scraped some cream off the side of his face and stuck her finger in her mouth.

"I don't think you are. You obviously enjoy doing this."

Sydney reached over with her index finger and scraped some off his chin, sticking it in her mouth. "Yummy. You know this never would have happened if you had given me the eclair in the first place. I thought you had learned your lesson on the cruise."

He grabbed a couple of napkins and wiped his face clean. "The only thing I learned on the cruise was that you were someone I couldn't live without."

"That's the sweetest thing anyone has ever said to me." She leaned over and kissed him. "Even sweeter than the eclair." She frowned. "Too bad we can't eat it now."

He grinned and leaned over toward the ice chest, pulling out another plastic bag. "I had a feeling this would happen, so I brought a backup."

Sydney blinked twice. "Another eclair?"

He nodded. "The other one was a stunt double. This is the real one. And it's just for you, my love." He handed her the bag.

She smiled and pulled the eclair from the bag. She was

about to take a bite and stopped. "Sure you don't want a bite?"

He shook his head. "Enjoy it."

Sydney leaned over and kissed him. "Thank you, Mr. Martin." She rubbed her tummy. "And Oscar Junior thanks you."

He shook his head. "It's going to be a girl. And I hope she's just as feisty as you."

THE END
****

Ready for more fun?
Go to the next page for
your **FREE** romantic comedy!

FREE romantic comedy!
All of my newsletter subscribers
get a free copy of my fun story,
Happy to be Stuck with You, plus
updates on new releases and sales.
http://www.richamooi.com/newsletter.

You can also browse my entire list of
romantic comedies on Amazon here:
Author.to/AmazonRichAmooi

ACKNOWLEDGMENTS

First, I would like to give a shout-out to my fans around the world. Thank you! It means the world to me that you read my books and it still blows me away that I can do this for a living. Thank you for all of the wonderful reviews on Amazon and Goodreads! Your letters and messages motivate me and help me write faster, so please send me an email to say hello. I personally reply to everyone. My address is rich@richamooi.com.

So many people helped to make this book possible and I'd like to take a moment to say thanks and acknowledge them here.

To my hot Spanish wife (author Silvi Martin). You're the best wife in the world and I would not be able to write these books without you. Thank you for your love and support and countless kisses. I love you.

To my editor, Mary Yakovets. Thanks again for making me look good!

A BIG thank you to Paula Bothwell and Sherry Stevenson for proofreading.

To my artist, Sue Traynor, who drew the fun cover. You rock! Love, love, love this cover and I appreciate your work tremendously.

To authors Becky Monson, Whitney Dineen, Tammi Labrecque, and Deb Julienne for your help. Thank you so much!

To all of the amazingly-talented authors in the super-secret Facebook AC group. Thank you for brainstorming with me.

To everyone at RWA, Chicklit Chat, and Indiepubclub. Thank you!

To my beta readers . . . Silvi, Isabel, Krasimir, Julita, Deb, Robert, and Maché. Your feedback is invaluable. It's amazing how much different the story is from first draft to final draft. It's because of you. Thank you for taking the time to help.

ABOUT THE AUTHOR

Rich Amooi is a former Silicon Valley radio personality and wedding DJ who now writes romantic comedies full-time. He is happily married to a kiss monster imported from Spain. Rich believes in public displays of affection, silliness, infinite possibilities, donuts, gratitude, laughter, and happily ever after.

Connect with Rich!
www.richamooi.com
rich@richamooi.com